"We can't do this, Alex."

He blinked and looked at Fran with a dazed expression. "I thought we were pulling it off rather well." His breathing was ragged and fast.

"Way too well," she agreed, stepping out of the circle of his arms. "But we have to forget this ever happened. This is a recipe for disaster. Mixing business with—"

"Pleasure is the word you're looking for," he supplied.

"Whatever you want to call it, we're asking for trouble if we don't stop. We've already established that you're not looking for love and neither am I."

Finally he said, "I suppose you're right. This isn't a good idea."

Fran felt a sharp pain in the region of her heart. Surely it was for the best? But since when did being right, or doing what was for the best, hurt so much?

Dear Reader,

Although the anniversary is over, Silhouette Romance is still celebrating our coming of age—we'll soon be twenty-one! Be sure to join us each and every month for six emotional stories about the romantic journey from first time to forever.

And this month we've got a special Valentine's treat for you! Three stories deal with the special holiday for true lovers. Karen Rose Smith gives us a man who asks an old friend to *Be My Bride?* Teresa Southwick's latest title, *Secret Ingredient: Love,* brings back the delightful Marchetti family. And Carla Cassidy's *Just One Kiss* shows how a confirmed bachelor is brought to his knees by a special woman.

Amusing, emotional and oh-so-captivating Carolyn Zane is at it again! Her latest BRUBAKER BRIDES story, *Tex's Exasperating Heiress,* features a determined groom, a captivating heiress and the pig that brought them together. And popular author Arlene James tells of *The Mesmerizing Mr. Carlyle,* part of our AN OLDER MAN thematic miniseries. Readers will love the overwhelming attraction between this couple! Finally, *The Runaway Princess* marks Patricia Forsythe's debut in the Romance line. But Patricia is no stranger to love stories, having written many as Patricia Knoll!

Next month, look for appealing stories by Raye Morgan, Susan Meier, Valerie Parv and other exciting authors. And be sure to return in March for a new installment of the popular ROYALLY WED tales!

Happy reading!

Mary-Theresa Hussey

Mary-Theresa Hussey
Senior Editor

Please address questions and book requests to:
Silhouette Reader Service
U.S.: 3010 Walden Ave., P.O. Box 1325, Buffalo, NY 14269
Canadian: P.O. Box 609, Fort Erie, Ont. L2A 5X3

Secret
Ingredient: Love

TERESA SOUTHWICK

SILHOUETTE *Romance*®

Published by Silhouette Books

America's Publisher of Contemporary Romance

SILHOUETTE BOOKS

ISBN 0-373-19495-1

SECRET INGREDIENT: LOVE

Visit Silhouette at www.eHarlequin.com

Printed in U.S.A.

Books by Teresa Southwick

Silhouette Romance

*Wedding Rings and Baby
  Things* #1209
The Bachelor's Baby #1233
**A Vow, a Ring, a Baby
  Swing* #1349
*The Way to a Cowboy's
  Heart* #1383
*And Then He Kissed Me #1405
*With a Little T.L.C. #1421
The Acquired Bride #1474
*Secret Ingredient: Love #1495

*The Marchetti Family

Silhouette Books

The Fortunes of Texas
Shotgun Vows

TERESA SOUTHWICK

is a native Californian who has recently moved to Texas.
Living with her husband of twenty-five years and two
handsome sons, she is surrounded by heroes. Reading
has been her passion since she was a girl. She couldn't
be more delighted that her dream of writing full-time
has come true. Her favorite things include: holding a
baby, the fragrance of jasmine, walks on the beach, the
patter of rain on the roof and, above all, happy endings.

Teresa also writes historical romance novels under the
same name.

BROCCOLI LASAGNA

12 oz lasagna noodles—wide
2 tbsp salad oil
1 1/2 tsp salt
1/4 tsp pepper
20 oz frozen broccoli (or spinach)
1 lb creamed cottage cheese
1/4 cup sour cream
2-3 cups tomato sauce
12 oz mozzarella cheese, grated

Cook noodles according to directions on package.
Drain, then toss with oil, salt and pepper until well
coated. Cook broccoli according to package directions.
Drain. Combine cottage cheese and sour cream and set
aside. Arrange enough noodles to cover bottom of an
8"x12" baking dish. Cover with half the broccoli and
some tomato sauce, then a layer of mozzarella cheese.
Add another layer of noodles, topped with broccoli,
tomato sauce and mozzarella cheese, and then add all of
the cottage cheese mixture. Top with remaining noodles
and a final layer of tomato sauce to cover. Sprinkle with
remaining mozzarella cheese. In a preheated 350°F oven,
bake for 30 minutes, until cheese melts and is golden on
top.

Chapter One

The way to a man's heart is through his stomach.

As she finished cleaning her kitchen, Fran Carlino thought about the nightly phone call and her mother's final irritating words. Fran wasn't looking for the way to a man's heart. She wasn't looking for a man. Period.

She turned the light out before flopping in her favorite worn chair in her apartment living room. She was tired. It had been a long day. A trained chef, she was finishing up her contract to develop natural baby food for a national company. That was good. Except it meant that she had to line up something else. Soon. She liked what she did, but freelancing was unstable and insecure—especially when it was time to pay bills.

Consulting was only a temporary divergence, a choice she'd made because she'd learned the hard way how tough the food service business was on a woman. In cooking school, she'd been flattered when the best looking guy picked her to romance. But it turned out that he'd been using her to further his career. He'd only wanted the secret ingredient to a recipe of hers that had impressed the teachers. One bruised, battered and filleted heart later, she had vowed that love was an ingredient that had no place in any kitchen. Or in her life.

Her ultimate goal was a restaurant of her own, where she called the shots.

Pulling out the Sunday classifieds, she flipped through, then stopped at the restaurant listings. After spreading the sheets out on the ottoman in front of her, she grabbed her red pen from the glass-topped table beside her. She started marking the want ads, although nothing very exciting was available.

"That's okay," she said to herself. "Something will turn up."

The doorbell rang, startling her. She wasn't expecting anyone.

She stood and hurried to the front door, pulling over her step stool to see out the peephole. The man was tall, dark-haired and carrying no weapons that she could see. Must be a salesman. She decided to answer, because it felt rude to ignore someone even if she wasn't buying what he was selling. And—her father would have used this as an example of why she needed a man to take care of her—he was wearing wire-rimmed glasses.

She got off her stool and opened the door as wide as the latched chain would let her. In spite of what her father thought, she wasn't a complete airhead just by virtue of being a woman. "Yes?"

"Fran Carlino?" the stranger asked.

"Yes?"

"I'd like to talk to you."

"That's what all the serial killers say," she answered. "Or salesmen. I'll cut to the chase, the part where I tell you I'm not interested in what you're selling. And I don't want to waste your time when you could be talking to someone who is interested. Goodbye," she said, closing the door.

He stuck his foot in the way. "Wait. I'm not a salesman. I have something to give you."

"Like I said, that's what they all say." She met his gaze. "Now let me close my door or I'll—"

"I'm Alex Marchetti."

"Good for you." The name sounded familiar, but she couldn't place it.

In her narrowed field of vision, he held out a paper shopping bag from a well-known department store. "My sister, Rosie Schafer, asked me to return these jars."

Rosie was her bookstore-owner friend who was test-marketing her baby food on her daughter, Stephanie. Her son, Joey, was still nursing. Rosie had mentioned her brothers, but she'd never said a word about how good-looking this one was. Fran was about to remove the chain from her door when that last thought stopped her. The phrase "beware of Greeks bearing gifts" flashed through her mind. Alex was Italian and holding baby food jars, but the same warning applied.

"You didn't have to bring them to me," she said. "I told Rosie I'd stop by the store to pick them up."

"Technically, I haven't actually given them to you. If you'll open up, I could do that."

"Just leave the bag in front of the door," she said. Fran couldn't decide whether to curse or bless her father for the years of cynicism conditioning that was now second nature to her. Her own unfortunate experience had reenforced his message, making her wary of men. "I'll get them later."

"You're not afraid of me, are you?"

Yes, she thought, but not for the reason he meant.

"How do I know you're who you say you are?" she asked, stalling.

"Instead of trying to tell you, I'll go straight for a positive ID and show you." He pulled out his wallet and handed her his driver's license through the small opening.

The Department of Motor Vehicles picture definitely matched him, not to mention that it was better than most people took with a professional photographer. But it was hard to miss with such great raw material. The description said he was six feet two, a hundred and ninety pounds, with dark brown hair and brown eyes.

"You're definitely Alex Marchetti."

"So are you going to open the door and let me do my good deed? If that's not enough to convince you, I've got a proposition."

"My father warned me about stuff like that." About a hundred million times he'd warned her. And where Leonardo Carlino left off, her four brothers began.

"I was referring to a job."

That piqued her interest. She did remember Rosie saying that her family owned a chain of restaurants. Since she was going to be out of work soon, what did she have to lose?

"Okay. We can talk. But you have to move your foot first." When he did, she shut the door long enough to unlatch the chain, then swung it wide. "Come in."

"Thanks."

"So talk to me," she said, shutting the door behind him.

"My sister says you're a trained chef with a flair for picking just the right ingredient to enhance a recipe," Alex began. He set the bag of jars down next to the door. "She claims that you can even make Brussels sprouts palatable."

"I'm proud to say that I haven't had a baby complain yet," she quipped.

He grinned and Fran nearly lost her balance. The wattage in his very attractive smile could put a twenty-four-hour-glow in a girl's heart. Maybe even forty-eight, she thought, absorbing the warmth. Correction: any girl but her. But even she had to admit that he was a walking, talking poster boy for tall, dark and handsome. He made the glasses look macho—sexy, in fact. He even made his wrinkled, pinstriped slacks and rumpled white dress shirt look good. Especially because his long sleeves were rolled up, revealing wide, strong forearms sprinkled with dark hair. It was a look that she was especially vulnerable to. And Alex wore it better than any man she'd ever seen.

Because of her very powerful feminine response to him, she was about to thank him for returning the jars, then politely ask him to leave. But he hadn't told her about the job yet. "I was just going to have some tea. Would you like a cup? Or are you a coffee kind of guy?"

"Nothing, thanks."

He followed her through her living room to her small kitchen. The U-shaped work area included a bar. Alex stood on the other side of it while she put on the tea-kettle. From the corner of her eye, she watched him look around. The Marchettis owned a very successful chain of restaurants. Her small but cozy surroundings had to be a world away from wherever he hung his hat.

He put his hands in his pockets. "My sister tells me that you're a food consultant. She says the baby food you've developed is great. My niece loves it."

"I have to take her word for that. Unfortunately, I don't get direct feedback—you'll pardon the pun— from my little consumers."

She met his gaze, and the wry look on his face told her he got the second play on words that she'd managed to slip in. She couldn't help liking that about him. To dim the tractor beam of his appeal, she turned her back on him and reached up into the cupboard for her sugar container. "What else did Rosie tell you?"

Behind her, Alex cleared his throat. "That you have good taste."

"How nice of her." Fran turned around in time to see his lowered gaze size her up from top to bottom. That and the appreciative look in his eyes made her wonder if brother and sister had been discussing food at the time. It also made her heart skip into an escalated rhythm. Setting her sugar on the counter, she said, "Do you concur?"

"I haven't tasted your cooking," he said, his voice husky. "But your apartment is charming."

"Thank you," she answered, annoyed at the breathless quality that had crept into her own voice without warning. "I tried to give it touches that reflect myself. Why do I get the feeling that Rosie wasn't talking about food *or* furnishings when she said I had good taste?"

One dark eyebrow rose. "She didn't mention how perceptive you are. As a matter of fact, she launched into a Fran Carlino monologue, including that you're five feet two, but no eyes of blue. Instead they're..." he met her gaze "...cocoa-brown. Rosie said they're big and gorgeous, and I'd have to concur. She also said you're concise, and curvy and cute as a—''

"If you say button, I'm going to have to throw you out," Fran interrupted.

"Okay. Although she did, and that was when I asked what all of that had to do with your cooking."

"So she did actually tell you about my cooking."

He nodded. "She said that the baby food you're developing is simple and pure, for children prone to allergies. I was just wondering if you'd done anything else?"

"I worked on a line of fat-free muffins. After that I developed recipes for dry soup mix. I also did some frozen vegetable stir-fry, just add beef or chicken."

"What about preservatives in the baby food?"

"It's pretty easy to prepare without additives, then freeze. To test-market, I gave it to Rosie in jars, but we're working on the packaging this week. So far the advance reports are good. The secret is simplicity. I don't get too free with spices that might be disaster to their immature systems."

"Sounds like a smart move. Too many sleepless nights with a baby battling indigestion could generate some pretty negative publicity."

Fran put a cup and saucer on the counter, then added a tea bag. "Do you know a lot about publicity?"

He nodded. "I'm vice president in charge of marketing as well as R and D for Marchetti's Inc."

"Research and development," she said, feeling an "aha" moment coming on. "So there is an actual job? And Rosie really did send you over?"

"Sort of. But it's more in the category of a double whammy," he said, without batting an eye.

"Double. As in two. I'm intrigued. What's whammy number one?" she asked.

"I'm looking for just the right person to oversee my latest research and development plan for Marchetti's Inc. Rosie tells me you're an excellent chef."

"I went to culinary school," Fran said. "Right now I'm doing freelance work. But you already know that."

He nodded. "I need a food consultant to develop a line of frozen foods. I want to take the Marchetti's menu into as many homes across America as possible."

The teakettle shrilled and she lifted it off the stove, then poured steaming water into her cup. Fran looked at him. "That's an exciting proposition," she said.

He nodded. "I intend to carve a niche in frozen foods for the company. Are you aware that it's a four-billion-dollar-a-year industry?"

No, but she was aware of how incredibly good-looking he was when he turned earnest and intense. "That's a lot of frozen peas and carrots," she conceded.

"Exactly. I think the time is optimum to branch out into another venue with the right product. Our father started the first Marchetti's Restaurant. When he retired, my older brother, Nick, took over the company and expanded it, creating the present restaurant chain. I plan to do the same, just in a different direction."

She leaned her elbows on the counter between them and rested her chin in her hand. "Second-son syndrome."

"Excuse me?"

"You're suffering from second-son syndrome. In the Middle Ages, the first son inherited the castle and son number two played second fiddle, twiddling his thumbs because he had nothing to do. Nick took Marchetti's into the fast lane and you're saying, 'Hey, notice me, too.'"

Alex frowned. "There's only one thing wrong with that theory."

"And that would be?"

"I'm the third son."

"Ah. Any sons after one and two get paid to do nothing. That makes the syndrome twice as acute."

Why did she feel this absurd desire to tease him? Maybe because he was so serious. A side effect of the glasses. But mostly because she found her almost instant attraction to him disconcerting. Whatever the reason, she couldn't resist the urge to loosen him up a little.

"Did you say I'm twice as cute?"

Mission accomplished, she thought, watching him struggle to hold back a grin. "No. I said the syndrome is *acute* times two for son number three. You're competing with two brothers for approval, affection and your rightful place in the castle dynamics."

Alex watched as she dunked her tea bag. She wouldn't blame him if he grabbed it away and stuffed it somewhere. Like in her mouth. This wasn't the first time her mouth had gotten her into hot water. She had a feeling it wouldn't be the last, either.

She put her soggy tea bag on her saucer. Then she stirred some sugar into the steaming liquid while she waited for him to respond to her last verbal barb.

"I think your theory is interesting," he finally said. "And there may be a grain of truth to it."

"Really?" she asked. She'd expected him to bristle and get angry. Not to semi-agree with her.

"If second-son syndrome means that I want my parents and brothers to be as proud of me as I am of them, then I'm guilty as charged.''

''Hmm.'' She could relate to that. She felt the same way. Only in her case it wasn't likely to happen. She wrapped her hands around her mug and blew into the steam to cool off the liquid. ''Good luck with your goal,'' she said.

''Do you have siblings, Fran?''

''Do I have siblings?'' She laughed. ''Do four older brothers qualify?''

The corners of his very attractive mouth turned up. ''No wonder you and Rosie hit it off.''

She nodded. ''We did bond over the trials and tribulations of having a father and four stand-in bodyguards.''

''So you've been able to observe second-son syndrome firsthand,'' he commented.

''Among other things.''

''Like what?''

''Like marriage and kids. For women, it's not much evolved from a feudal society.''

''How do you figure?''

She sipped her tea, then said, ''Think about it. The woman works her fingers to the bone fetching for her husband and sons, and all she gets is a place to live, food and clothes.''

''Don't you think that's a little harsh?'' he asked. ''My mother and sister seem to find family, especially motherhood, very rewarding.''

''I'm exaggerating a little. But from my firsthand observations, it seems more servitude than satisfying. I keep after my mother to get a life, but she insists that she has one, thank you very much. But I don't see that she's receiving enough personal fulfillment for me to follow in her footsteps. Much to my father's annoyance.''

"Why annoyance?"

"He believes a woman's place is in the home. Her fulfillment is taking care of a husband and children. He even wanted me to be a teacher.''

A shadow crossed Alex's face, and she wondered what she'd said to put it there.

"Why teaching?" he asked, the sad look chasing away the warmth in his dark eyes.

"Good career for a mom, because when you're finished with work, your children get out of school. Same vacations.''

"What's wrong with that?"

"For starters, it was his idea, not mine. And—''

He held up a hand to stop her. "This sounds like a long, yet interesting story. Would you mind if we sat down?" he asked.

"Of course not. How thoughtless of me.''

She wasn't usually so rude. But apparently her brain was on overload, filled as it was with good-looking Alex Marchetti. After that, there wasn't a whole lot of room left over for rational thought, not to mention manners. Then she'd climbed on her soapbox, something that usually followed when the subject of her family came up. Everything else went out the window. Including courtesy.

She waved her hand toward the living room. "Please.''

He turned away and she couldn't help peeking at him from the rear. For a while now, Fran had wondered about the hoopla, hype and hyperbole associated with men's backsides. Movies, magazines and other media were full of it. And she didn't get it. At least she hadn't until this very moment. It was sort of comforting to know she wasn't immune.

He filled out a pair of slacks in the best possible way. She would bet he was something of a phenomenon in a pair of worn jeans. Alex Marchetti probably sat behind a desk all day, and it wasn't fair that he showed not a single hint of secretary spread. More proof that God was a man.

He sighed as he settled his very attractive rear end in her big, overstuffed chair. Her want ads still rested on the ottoman in front of him. "This is comfortable," he said.

"I think so, too. It was my grandmother's." Fran sat on the sofa at a right angle to him. "She died a couple years ago." She smiled sadly.

"I guess she was very special to you."

Fran nodded. "My father's mother. She visited all the time. We were very close. She financed my rebellion."

"Rebellion?"

"Culinary school. My father refused to pay for it. He said that if I liked to cook, I should get married and prepare meals for one man instead of a bunch of strangers."

"Hmm," was his only comment. "Where did you go to school?"

"San Francisco."

He lifted one eyebrow. "Chalk one up for your grandmother. And you still miss her."

"Every day," Fran agreed. "But that's why I love that chair. It's nice to have something to remind me of her."

"Do you want me to give you my amateur psychological take on that?"

"Nope. And I won't practice armchair psychology if you won't."

"You already have," he said wryly.

"Okay. No more cracks about second-son syndrome."

He held out his hand. "Deal."

"Done," she agreed, slipping her hand into his.

A tingle of awareness skittered through her. If she had foreseen the magnitude of disturbance caused by the warmth of his large hand, she would have kept hers to herself.

She removed her fingers from his, hoping he didn't notice her abruptness. It smacked of attraction. She didn't want to be attracted to him. Nothing personal. But after her disaster, she wasn't interested in a flirtation or anything more serious with any man. Especially one in the food service industry. If only Alex didn't look so darn cute sitting in her grandmother's chair. What in the world had possessed her to look through that peephole in the first place? Curiosity.

Which reminded her. She was still curious about the second reason he'd dropped by. He'd admitted he was looking for a chef, but he didn't seem terribly impressed with her verbal credentials. There wasn't much chance he would offer her the job. Too bad. It was a wonderful opportunity.

But he'd said he was here for two reasons, and he'd only accounted for one. "So what's the second whammy?" she asked.

"Excuse me?"

"You said you're here because of a double whammy. Chef search is number one. What's number two?"

"Matchmaking."

Chapter Two

"Why would you assume Rosie was matchmaking?" Fran asked. "Because I'm a *female* chef?"

"Yes."

Alex didn't miss the defensive note in her voice or the way her gaze narrowed at his response. He'd been around the restaurant business long enough to know that women who decided on this career had a tough time. Attitudes were changing, but males still dominated the kitchens in a lot of four star restaurants.

He couldn't resist adding, "If you were a guy, it would have been the single whammy."

"Huh?"

"Chef search. No matchmaking."

She nodded slowly as the corners of her mouth curved in a knowing smile. "Okay. But why would your sister try to fix you up?"

"Because she's a hopeless romantic."

"I wouldn't think a guy who looks like you would have trouble finding a woman on his own."

She offered the observation without embarrassment or evasiveness. A woman on the make wouldn't be so straightforward. He found her refreshing.

And more, he thought. Sweat broke out on his forehead as she touched a finger to her full bottom lip. He wondered how it would taste. That thought came out of nowhere. He'd never felt such a strong attraction. Not since Beth, he amended. Guilt hit him hard and fast. Followed by the pain—dull now, but still there, every time he thought about her and what they'd lost. Love like that happened only once in a lifetime. And fate, karma or whatever you wanted to call it had dumped on him in a big way. He'd found the perfect woman, but chance had stolen from him the part where they would grow old together. Fate wouldn't get another chance to kick him in the teeth.

"I'm not looking for a woman," he said. With luck, in addition to being direct, Fran wasn't inquisitive. This subject was off-limits. There was no point in discussing it.

Her eyes glittered, as if she wanted to ask more. But all she said was, "Then that's why Rosie is trying to fix you up. It's a delicious challenge. I just don't understand why she would think *I* was matchmaking material."

"There was that cute-as-a-button remark. Rosie said it, not me," he stated, raising his hands in surrender.

He had to admit Rosie had been right about that. Funny, he could see buttons as cute, but not sexy. And Fran Carlino had sex appeal in spades. Especially her mouth. Straight white teeth showed to perfection when she smiled, which she did often. She had full soft lips. Kissable lips.

"I would prefer stunning or drop-dead gorgeous to

cute, but at least she didn't tell you I need to wear a bag over my head in public.''

He blinked and forced himself to switch his focus from her mouth to the words coming out of it. "Actually, she was right about you. You're very attractive, Fran.''

"Be still my heart," she said, touching a hand to her chest. "Now there's a line to turn a woman's head. You really are out of practice. You're not kidding, are you—about not looking for a woman?''

"No." It wasn't even a matter of looking. He'd had his shot. It hadn't worked out. End of story.

"Then if you suspected Rosie was matchmaking, but you're not interested in participating, why are you here?''

"She said I couldn't get you. And if I wanted to know why, I had to ask you myself.''

"Ah," Fran said, with one emphatic nod that said she understood completely. "I get it. Brilliant strategy. And it worked like a charm.''

"What worked?''

"Reverse psychology.''

"What happened to no more amateur analyzing?'' he asked.

"I forgot," she admitted. "But this is too classic, too characteristic of reverse psychology.''

"How do you figure?''

"You're here, aren't you?''

"Unless this is the *Twilight Zone* it would be pointless to deny it. But I refuse to believe strategy played a part.''

"It's so obvious." She shook her head sympathetically. "Guys always want what they can't have. If anyone knows about this it's me. With four brothers, I've had lots of practice studying how the male mind works.''

"And how is that?''

"It has something to do with that whole prehistoric hunter-gatherer thing. Deny them, and they'll go out with single-minded determination and intense focus to hunt it down and bring it back to the cave. So Rosie's method worked. She said you couldn't bag me. Now you're here, spear in hand.'' She watched him for a moment, then added, "So to speak.''

"You've been reading too many of the psychology books in Rosie's store.''

Instead of taking offense, she laughed. "Probably. No doubt it's nothing more than a man's competitive nature.''

He nodded. "I'll go along with that. So, I'll bite. Why can't I get you?'' That sounded way too personal. "As in why can't I get you to work for me?''

She set her empty teacup and saucer on the end table beside the sofa. As she leaned sideways, the lamp's glow highlighted the flush on her cheek. She'd noticed his double entendre.

When she didn't answer right away, he asked, "Do you have something against Italian cuisine? Either cooking or eating?''

She shook her head. "I love it.''

"So your schedule is tight? You've got more work than you can handle? You couldn't fit me in with a shoehorn?''

"Nope. After the baby food contract is satisfied, I'm up for grabs.''

Did she realize she'd lobbed a double entendre of her own? "Then you're taking some much needed time off,'' he suggested. "Haven't had a vacation in years?''

"Wrong again. In fact, just before you rang my doorbell, I was wondering where my next job was coming from. I had the want ads out, and marked a few things that looked promising."

He reached over and picked up her marked up classifieds. Looking at the ads she'd circled, he read, "'Experienced cook. Must know breakfast.'" He lowered the newspaper and met her gaze.

She shrugged. "I know breakfast. Never met one I didn't like."

He glanced at the paper again. "'Busy retirement resort seeks chef experienced in home-style volume production.'"

The corners of her tantalizing mouth turned up. "I lived in a home once, and believe you me, in my house you didn't learn anything if not cooking food in volume. The Carlino boys could put it away faster than you can say hot and hearty."

Another circled ad caught his eye. "'Accepting applications for grill and taco bar positions.' Isn't this beneath you?"

"It's honest work." Her mouth pulled tight.

"Seems to me your family would help out if you're strapped and between assignments for a while."

She shook her head. "I'd rather not."

"Why?" If he was in need, his family would be there for him, as Fran had said, faster than you could say hot and hearty.

"I can take care of myself."

He decided to leave it at that. Fran Carlino had a story and he didn't want to hear it. Nothing personal. This was all about business. "So you're actively looking for work," he concluded.

"Yes," she agreed.

They looked at each other and said at the same time, "Definitely matchmaking."

"With overtones of reverse psychology," Alex added. "And just to clarify—I *could* get you? To work for me, that is?"

"Make me an offer."

The first offer that came to mind had nothing to do with a job and everything to do with exploring the curve and circumference of her mouth. Hello! There it was again. That weird attraction, and it didn't seem to want to let up. The realization rocked him. It had been a while, but he was pretty sure he hadn't reacted so strongly to a woman, not even Beth. This was different. And it was something he didn't want to think about.

Pushing the feelings aside, he reminded himself he was here on business. And if he knew anything about anything, it was work. He'd buried himself in it to get through every day without Beth.

He stood up. "An offer is a little premature. I'd like to see a résumé and references. Then…"

"What?"

"Well, I'm not sure. This isn't normally my area of expertise. My brother Joe is in charge of human resources. He's the recruiter."

"So should I see him?" she offered, seeming relieved somehow.

Alex shook his head. "I'd like to handle this. Partly because it's my project, but mostly because my brother is getting married soon."

"When?"

"Valentine's Day."

"The only day of the year set aside for lovers," she said.

"Yes," he agreed.

"So you believe in love. You're just not looking for it yourself."

"That doesn't mean I don't appreciate the significance of the day for others," he clarified. Just not himself. "You probably have a guy to Valentine with," he guessed.

"No. But I think it would be very romantic as a wedding day."

He grinned. "That from the woman who would say Joe bagged a female and is in the process of dragging her—by the hair, I might add—back to his cave."

She smiled at him. "There's no keeping a steadfast hunter-gatherer down," she said. "Apparently it doesn't run in the family."

"How's that?"

"You're not looking for a woman," she reminded him.

"Right." He cleared his throat. "If I were in charge of recruiting, I would probably want to know what job experience you've had."

"Okay, I'll get you my résumé and work history."

He pulled his wallet from his back pocket and handed her a business card. "Here's the address."

"Thanks."

Fran stood before the reception desk at Marchetti's Inc. the following afternoon. It was late, after five, and she'd spent much of the day debating with herself. Should she play it cool and wait a week before getting Alex Marchetti her résumé? Or appear eager and needy by doing it right away? She finally reasoned that it didn't matter. The man had seen her want ads. He knew how needy she was.

Stopping at the building's information desk, she'd

explained that she was there to see Alex. The woman had buzzed his office to announce her, and had listened to his response.

"Mr. Marchetti will see you," she'd said. "Tenth floor," she'd added with a polite smile.

"Thank you."

Remembering his deep, resonant tones, Fran wondered how the woman could listen to that wonderful voice and remain impassive. On the phone, there was no distraction to mute the full power of it. Then again, the receptionist looked to be in her late fifties. Not to mention that there were a lot of offices. She probably didn't talk to him much.

Shaking her head at her silly musing, Fran walked past the reception area to the elevator and took it to his floor. When the doors opened, she walked out and scanned the U-shaped desk and the woman behind it. Alex's secretary.

That explained it. The information lady probably only talked to his secretary. Hence her demeanor was safe and secure.

"I'm here to see Alex Marchetti," Fran explained to the gray-haired woman. With her cap of curls, she reminded Fran of one of the flitting fairy godmothers from the classic cartoon fairy tale.

Fran had to conclude that if Alex had had any say in hiring his secretary and the information lady, he had deliberately surrounded himself with females unavailable to him. He wasn't kidding about not looking for a woman. Fran couldn't help wondering why. A hunk like him could probably have anyone he wanted, but he'd taken himself out of circulation. She wasn't the only one with a long, yet interesting story. But she recalled the sadness in his brown eyes and had a suspicion his didn't have a happy ending.

"He's expecting you," the older woman said with a smile. "His office is down the hall to your left."

"Thanks," Fran said.

She quickly found his door, and knocked.

"Come in."

There was the voice. She took a deep, bracing breath, then entered his office. Alex sat behind the desk. Today he had on a tie, a paisley print in shades of brown and gold complementing his tan shirt. The long sleeves were rolled up. She couldn't suppress one small, appreciative sigh.

"Hi," she said.

"Hi," he answered. "What can I do for you?"

She clutched her portfolio briefcase tightly. "Here I am, as promised."

"I wasn't expecting you so soon. Anytime this week would have been fine."

"I thought you were anxious to get started."

"And I thought you were busy finishing up your current assignment."

"Just tying up loose ends," she explained, struggling for perky.

His words made her stomach fall like the sudden drop on a roller coaster. He didn't want her. The thought flashed through her mind, and disappointment quickly followed. She couldn't tell whether she was disturbed professionally or personally. That sent her to a whole different level of emotional confusion. She'd been involved with a guy who had dumped her *after* he got what he wanted. She hadn't done anything for Alex yet. Her self-esteem would plummet to the basement if she were jettisoned without even being on board.

"Have a seat." He indicated one of the two leather chairs in front of his desk.

"Thanks." She sat down and crossed one leg over the other, hearing the whisper of her nylons. She noticed Alex glance in that direction, but was pretty sure his desk blocked his view. And she was glad about that.

On top of her debate about whether or not to show up at all, she'd had a hard time deciding what to wear. It was December in southern California, but unseasonably warm. Should she show up in a suit with a skirt that was businesslike yet feminine, or a pantsuit that was professional and didn't draw too much attention to her as a woman? Based on their meeting the previous evening, she hadn't been able to decide whether he was retro or progressive on that last point.

She'd finally chosen an outfit that made *her* feel professional and confident. Her chocolate-brown suit filled the bill nicely. Its not-too-short skirt and the fitted jacket that hugged her hips and stopped about six inches from her hem made her feel good.

He stared at her for several moments, then finally said, "May I see your résumé?"

"Of course." She quickly unzipped her briefcase and removed a folder. "I also have letters of recommendation from each of the companies I've worked with."

Alex scanned the sheets, giving her a chance to scan him. As he concentrated, frown lines appeared between his dark brows. He had a well-formed nose and a nice mouth. Very nice, she thought with a little shiver. His cheeks and jaw sported a five o'clock shadow. Incredibly male with just a hint of danger, she decided. But the wire-rimmed glasses debunked that impression pretty quickly. His wrists were wide, dusted with a masculine covering of dark hair, and his hands, with their long fingers, looked lean and strong.

"Very impressive," he said.

"Yes, indeed." She gave herself a mental shake and, with an effort, switched gears back to business. She cleared her throat. "They seemed to be happy with my work."

He set the last letter on top of the folder. "With a health-conscious consumer public, the fat-free muffin mix is very timely. So is the frozen vegetable stir-fry."

"Not to mention the recipe booklet for the dried soup mix," she reminded him. "I included hints to cut fat and calories."

"I see," he said, looking at her. Was that appreciation in his eyes?

Maybe. But that didn't dismiss his vague tone. She would bet her double boiler that he had mega-reservations about hiring her.

"Why do I hear a 'but' in your voice?" she asked.

"You have no experience in entrées."

"Not as a consultant, that's true. But as my résumé states, I was trained at a prestigious culinary school. Making entrées was part of the curriculum. I know which ingredients freeze well."

Alex met her gaze. "I was hoping to find someone with more—"

"Seasoning?" she questioned when he hesitated.

The corners of his mouth turned up slightly. "Frankly, yes," he said.

Tamping down her disappointment, she asked, "How long have you been looking?"

"Awhile now," he admitted. "Casually at first, because I was fleshing out the idea and brainstorming the ad campaign. I had a verbal agreement with a chef, but he bailed out on me when he got an offer for his own restaurant. So when I found myself back at square one, I started looking at our own personnel in the restaurants, without pressuring anyone."

"And?"

He shook his head. "No dice."

"Then what?" she asked.

"I was hoping to land a well-known name in the business, but that went nowhere. I also talked to culinary schools. I interviewed some students who came highly recommended."

"Apparently that didn't go well?"

He shook his head. "Either they were starstruck, with ambitions of working at world-famous restaurants in New York, or their specialties leaned toward froufrou and artsy."

"Not on the same wavelength?" she asked, adding a dollop of understanding to her tone.

"That's putting it mildly." He leaned forward and folded his hands, resting them on his desk.

She tried, but couldn't summon sincere sympathy. Not when she wanted this job so much. She couldn't help feeling grateful that he was having a difficult time filling the position. It boded better for her.

"I hate to say this, but it sounds like you don't have a lot of choices left," she said.

"You noticed." He sighed as he ran his fingers through his dark hair. "Look, Fran, I worked through lunch and I'm starving. What would you say to an early dinner? The very first Marchetti's Restaurant my father opened is across the street. Would you care to join me?"

Part of her wanted to say, "Lead me to the linguine." The other part said her presence here at all was the main ingredient in a recipe for trouble. But she needed a job. And this assignment was leaps and bounds better than grill and taco bar positions. Her only concern was Alex Marchetti. He didn't seem like the type who would turn the project over to even the most experienced chef, which she was not. That meant he would be a hands-on employer. Shivering at the thought, she reminded herself his hands wouldn't be on her. This was work, not personal. The business of cooking had been personal once and she'd promised herself that she wouldn't ever let it be again.

This instant and powerful attraction to a man had never happened to her before. She was guessing, but felt it had something to do with the fact that Alex had dropped by without warning last night. She hadn't had time to erect her defenses. He'd slipped past her fortifications before she could arm herself against his arsenal of looks, laughs and loads of sex appeal.

But she couldn't let a little thing like that stop her. If she was the type to run from confrontation, she would be a teacher today instead of a chef.

"A business dinner would be fine, Alex. I'd like very much to check out Marchetti's menu."

"You've never been to one of our restaurants?"

She shook her head. "Sorry."

He stood up. "It's time we rectified that."

"Hi, Abby." Alex gave his newest sister-in-law a kiss on the cheek.

He and Fran had just entered the restaurant. As assistant manager, Abby happened to be filling in for the hostess. He didn't miss the look on Fran's face. Her expression registered surprise, disapproval and a distinct "Do I really want to work for a guy who kisses his employees?"

"A table for two, Alex?" Abby asked, smiling politely at Fran. Her blue eyes glittered with curiosity.

Alex had always thought the penchant for meddling was an inherited Marchetti trait. Apparently it was passed on through marriage, he realized as his blond sister-in-law gave Fran a thorough once-over. But in all fairness, Abby wasn't accustomed to seeing him with a woman. And there was something about Fran— a sparkle, a sense of fun humming through her, a subtle sexiness.

He cleared his throat. "A quiet table please, Ab. We have business to discuss," he added quickly. Squash the rumors before they got started. No sense fueling the family gossip mill. The meddling Marchettis needed no challenge or encouragement.

"I have the perfect table," Abby answered.

He looked at Fran, the doubtful expression in her eyes reminding him he hadn't made introductions. "Fran Carlino, I'd like you to meet Abby Marchetti. She and Nick have been married..." He stopped to think how long it had been.

"Six months, and we're still on our honeymoon," Abby stated with stars in her eyes. "But who's counting? It's nice to meet you, Fran."

"My pleasure," Fran said, visibly relaxing.

"I've got a corner booth, quiet and secluded." Abby led the way through the romantically lit, almost empty restaurant. "You picked a good time to come in, Alex. The dinner rush hasn't started yet."

"Good."

His sister-in-law seated them. "I'll send the waiter

over. Enjoy your dinner. Good to see you, Alex,'' she said, then she was gone.

He knew she'd wanted to say, "Good to see you with a woman." He wished his family would get over worrying about him being alone. They would have a field day if he told them that visions of Fran kept popping into his mind. Followed quickly by a nagging feeling that he'd done something wrong. He pushed that thought away. He wished his caring but misguided relatives would find another charity case. He'd been taking care of himself—alone—for a while now. And he'd been doing a pretty good job of it if he did say so himself. That reminded him of something Fran had said that he'd wondered about.

Alex looked at her across the table. "Before we talk business, would you mind explaining the remark you made last night? About being able to take care of yourself?"

"Why do you want to know?"

"Curiosity. You were a shade defensive." He shrugged. "I just wondered why you would feel you couldn't count on your family."

"I can count on them. I just choose not to. Because I would hear about how if I was married, I wouldn't have to ask them for help because I'd have a man to take care of me."

"And you don't want a man in your life?"

"That's oversimplifying."

"How?"

She clasped her hands together and rested her forearms on the table. "My family is big on following in footsteps. My four brothers followed my father into the construction business. A lot like your family. The difference is yours seems to accept Rosie's decision to be an independent businesswoman.''

"Your family hasn't accepted your career?''

She shook her head. "I don't think my father knows what to do with me. He's never gotten over the fact that I wasn't a boy. Plus girls can't work construction. I was supposed to do what my mother did—marry and have babies. He wants me to find a man so he won't have to worry about me anymore. I feel a lot like the Olympic torch, getting handed off to become someone else's responsibility." She sighed. "He would want me in a nunnery if he knew about the jerk in cooking school. But that's a sad, boring story," she said, looking as if she would like to call back those words.

Alex laughed. "What's wrong with allowing someone the privilege of looking after you?''

"I'm not a responsibility. I can take care of myself. A man would quadruple the home-front workload. My career would suffer.''

"And your career is important to you?''

"You bet your corporate office it is. I love what I do. A good thing, since culinary school was no picnic for a woman. I didn't go through that so I could play second fiddle to a guy and his laundry.''

"So a job with Marchetti's is important to you?''

She nodded. "You said it yourself. I don't have experience with entrées. This job would give me that and, with a little luck, put me on a course closer to my ultimate goal.''

"Which is?''

"A restaurant of my own." She met his gaze. "You're wondering why I've taken a detour from that.''

"Yeah." She'd read his mind. He hoped she

couldn't read the rest of his thoughts as easily. Or she would know how interested he was in her mouth and how it would feel and taste. He forced himself to concentrate on what she was saying.

"I'm sure you're aware that there's a certain prejudice against women in this business."

"I've seen some," he admitted.

"School was tough, but I was naive and thought when I finished it would be behind me. Unfortunately, I couldn't find a position I wanted in the restaurant field. When I was offered a consulting job, I took it, even though it veered away from my objective."

"So you want me to hire and train my competition?"

She laughed. "When you put it like that, it wouldn't be very smart. But realistically, my goal is quite a way down the road. And it doesn't matter what my future plans are. You need someone now. And I'm the best person for the job."

"You certainly are cocky."

"That implies you don't think I can do what I say."

He shook his head. "Let's just call me skeptical."

"So give me a chance to prove myself."

"That's tempting."

She frowned. "Let me ask you something now."

"Okay."

"Would your reluctance to hire me have anything to do with the fact that I'm a woman?"

Yes, he admitted to himself. But not for the reason she thought. There was something about Fran. She'd made him notice her. And he didn't want to notice any woman. But he was as dedicated to his career as she was to hers. He wasn't going to just turn this project over to her. He intended to oversee it. That meant he would see her—a lot. What would it be like to work closely with her?

But, as she'd pointed out, he was out of options. "No," he lied. "The fact that you're a woman in no way impacts my decision about whether or not to offer you the job."

"Then what's the problem?"

"You're inexperienced. I don't want to say no out of hand. But I'm not sure what my next step should be."

"I'll cook for you," she offered. "Let me put my money where my mouth is."

He'd like to put his mouth where her mouth was. That thought took him by surprise again. Who was he kidding? He wasn't surprised. He'd been semi-obsessed with her mouth since he'd met her almost twenty-four hours ago. And *that* was the main reason he hesitated to hire her.

"I thought your father didn't want you cooking for strange men," he said.

"Strangers," she clarified. "Besides, he doesn't get a vote. And I really want this job."

"Something to prove to your family?"

"Maybe. As I said, it *would* look great on my résumé. And the bottom line is you haven't found anyone yet. Time's awasting. I'm good at my job and I'd like the opportunity to prove it to you."

"Fair enough. When and where?"

"Tomorrow night. My apartment."

"I'll be there."

Chapter Three

This time Fran was ready for him. And getting ready for a man like Alex Marchetti was no small feat.

She didn't just mean ready as in food preparation and presentation, either. Although she had to admit she'd done herself proud. Surveying her modest circular oak table with the four surrounding ladder-back chairs, she nodded with satisfaction. A white linen cloth covered the small round surface. Her grandmother's flatware was arranged to leave space for her supermarket-special dishes. In her dollar-store water goblet, the cloth napkin fanned out, exotically folded the way she'd so painstakingly learned. And there was extra glassware on the table just to show that she knew how it should look.

In the center of everything was a vase filled with flowers from the grocery store hothouse. Rust-colored mums, yellow carnations, baby's breath and greens mingled their perfume with the aroma of her two favorite entrées. Presentation was as important as taste, and she'd done the very best she could with what she had for maximum visual appeal. Now her culinary skills had to stand on their own. For reasons she could neither understand nor explain, she wanted to impress Alex Marchetti. And, unfortunately, getting hired for the job wasn't her only motivation.

But dazzling Alex Marchetti with food and atmosphere wasn't the only thing she was ready for. Resisting his electric effect on her senses was going to be touchier than getting a soufflé to stand at attention. If she was right, and she was sure she was, he'd wowed her with the element of surprise.

She had told herself repeatedly that good looks and a physique that made her palms tingle to touch him were just *his* presentation. She had no intention of digging deeper to find out if his ingredients—looks, charm and temptation—blended into a dish with substance. He was dishy, all right, but she was on a restricted diet. Once burned, twice shy. So bring on his sex appeal, animal magnetism and magazine-cover backside. She wasn't afraid. She wasn't even tempted. She wasn't going to let anything, especially a good-looking man, come between her and the job she wanted.

She glanced at the clock on the stove. He was due at seven. It was six fifty-five. Her palms started to sweat and her stomach dropped as if she were in the first car on a roller coaster headed down the world's longest drop.

The doorbell sounded, making her jump. She took a deep breath and let it out as she surveyed her table one last time. She was grateful that he was punctual; she didn't think she could handle clock watching. Her nerves were already stretched as tight as the skin on a stuffed and trussed Thanksgiving turkey.

I am so ready, she said to herself as she walked through her living room toward the door, where she called, "Who is it?"

"Alex. Remember me? Your friendly, neighborhood serial killer."

She couldn't help laughing, in spite of the fact that his deep voice raised tingles that chased each other up and down her back. She took the chain off and opened the door. One look at Alex's worn, button-fly jeans and white shirt, sleeves rolled to just below his elbows, told her she was *not* ready.

"Hi," she said breathlessly. "Come in."

"Hi," he answered, walking through the door with a bottle cradled in each arm. "I brought some wine. One white, one red. I wasn't sure what you'd be serving."

"Thanks. But you didn't have to do that. This is a job interview." She grabbed the doorknob to steady herself when he grinned.

"I know. But it isn't like any interview I've ever conducted," he said.

"Preparing food isn't like any other job. You get results on the spot. Or not," she added.

"True." He sniffed. "Your results smell pretty good."

"I hope so. Let me show you to your table." She took the lead, then glanced over her shoulder. "This way, please."

They walked the short distance into her kitchen. She took the two bottles of wine from him and set them on the bar while he surveyed her efforts. Then he looked down at her, a slight frown marring his forehead just above the rims of his glasses.

"There's only one place setting. You're not joining me?"

"Every chef strives to imprint his or her own style," she said. "I'm going for the mystique. Joining the diner would shatter the atmosphere."

And component number one in her recipe for success in working for Alex was to keep her distance. Pretend she was head chef of her own restaurant, where she could make policy. In this case: stay as far from Alex Marchetti as she could. And she had to admit it was a good rule, because already this felt too much like an awkward first date.

"When I was growing up, there was an unspoken law—never let anyone eat alone." He rested his hands on lean, jean-clad hips as he met her gaze. "Or maybe you have another strategy. You're going to poison me and put me out of my second-son syndrome misery."

"Right. And I could kiss my cooking career good-bye."

"Or me."

"I beg your pardon?"

"You could kiss me." He looked as if he would like to take the words back. Shaking his head, he said, "Bad joke. But I'm serious about this. I think we should eat together."

"Haven't got time," she said. "You have to be judge, jury and executioner. While I'm hostess, wait staff and chef. Please take a seat. Course number one is coming up. I hope you're hungry."

"Starved."

As Alex uttered the single word, she caught a glimpse of the dark intensity in his eyes. She swore he was looking at her mouth like a famished man. Flutters started in her stomach and spread to her knees. As if she wasn't nervous enough! This was the best opportunity she'd ever had. It would be a real feather in her high, white chef's hat. All she had to do was not mess up. And that was a tall order, because her hands were shaking like a power line in a hurricane. She'd like to know which of the gods she'd inadvertently offended and give him a penance raincheck. This business was hard enough without the extra challenge of serving a flawless meal while under the influence of Alex Marchetti.

She smiled brightly. "A healthy appetite is a chef's best friend. I can show you to a table now, sir."

He rested his hand on one of the chairs and smiled wryly. "I think I can find it."

"You're not just another pretty face."

Before he could see how much she liked his face, she turned away, wishing he was a balding fifty-year-old who didn't know what hair color to put on his driver's license. But she'd seen his picture, not to mention the living, breathing man. His dark brown hair was wavy and thick, just begging to be touched. Focus! she ordered herself. In her professional capacity, she'd never had trouble doing that. Except for her one misstep in culinary school. Unfortunately, it was also a stumble of the heart. One she would never repeat.

Darn it, she wanted this job; she was a good chef. She needed to get Alex's attention. If the way to a man's heart was through his stomach, she'd have it nailed. The job, not the man, she amended.

"I prepared a variety of dishes, so you could see the range of my skills," she said, opening her refrigerator.

She pulled out a bowl of antipasto salad lavish with greens, cheese and black olives, and a more artsy arrangement of fresh spinach, asparagus and artichoke topped with alfalfa sprouts. Over the first she ladled a combination of spiced aromatic oil and estragon vinegar. She vigorously tossed the mixture, venting some of her nervous energy on the poor, innocent vegetables before placing a portion on a salad plate. On the other she spooned a delicate blend of light olive oil, garlic vinegar and her favorite combination of salad seasonings.

She set the two choices in front of him, along with a basket of fresh baked rolls wrapped in white linen to keep them warm.

"Enjoy," she said in her best professional voice. It would have been more businesslike without the husky quality, which made her sound like a call girl showcasing her attributes.

"This looks wonderful," he said, taking the salad fork and testing first one, then the other. He chewed thoughtfully. "It tastes as good as it looks. Both of them."

"Good." She went back into her work space. "I've got more courses, so save some room."

"Are you sure you can't sit down and eat some of this?"

"I'm not hungry. I've been tasting everything. A good chef does, you know."

"So I've been told."

Bald-faced lies, except statement number three. A good chef was *supposed* to taste as she went along. Unfortunately, Fran had a knot in her stomach the size of Los Angeles and couldn't get anything down. If she aced this interview, it would be because her instincts were in tip-top shape and she really and truly was an outstanding chef.

From the oven she removed a baking sheet and

placed the contents on a serving platter. Then she put the next course in the oven for heating. Rounding the bar, she set the platter on the table, then put one of the appetizers it held on his plate.

"Portobello mushrooms," she announced.

He sniffed, then tasted. "Excellent," he commented. "I don't think I've ever had better." He finished the whole thing.

"I'm glad you like it. Entrées will be ready in about ten minutes. I'll open some wine," she said, starting to turn away.

He stood up. "I'll do it. If you'll show me the way to the corkscrew."

Uh-oh. Red alert. He was changing the rules already. This was her kitchen and he was making himself at home. Familiarity breeds contempt. Down with friendly. Fie on familiar. Cool and distant. Up with professional and businesslike, and what had happened to that, anyway?

She looked up at him—way up. Clearing her throat, she said, "Do you always open the wine in a competitor's restaurant, Mr. Marchetti?"

"Since when are you a competitor? I thought we were on the same team."

"I'm trying out for a spot on the team. Remember?"

"Yeah. And I seem to recall you calling me Alex. What happened to that?"

"I'm being formal, putting my best professional foot forward. I just need a chance to show you what I can do."

There it was again. That breathless quality to her voice. Along with her call girl tone she was tossing double entendres like an antipasto salad. As her cheeks burned with embarrassment, she hoped he wouldn't attach a personal meaning to what she'd said. "If you can't stand the heat, get out of the kitchen" had never rung more true. And she'd been face-to-face with the saying more than once since she'd decided on a male-dominated career.

"Okay. You open the wine," he said. But he didn't sit down.

From one of her kitchen drawers, she removed a foil cutter and corkscrew. The first worked like a charm. Unfortunately, the second was inexpensive, antiquated, and only penetrated the cork. It didn't have handles on the sides to propel the stopper upward. She tried to pull it out, but didn't have the strength. Then she attempted to wiggle it loose, without luck.

Finally, Alex gently took the bottle from her. With only enough effort to cause a slight tightening in the tendons of his wide forearm, he removed the cork. "Voilà."

"I feel like a gymnast waiting to see how much the judges will deduct for a fall off the balance beam."

"Strength and manual dexterity are not the benchmarks of a good chef. I only deduct points for an entrée that triggers the gag reflex or food poisoning."

"You're joking, but this is very serious to me."

"In a restaurant setting the waiter or wine steward would wrestle with this bottle. Any muscle-bound moron can do it. It's not a failure."

"It's not a win, either."

"Lighten up. If your cooking tastes as good as it smells, you've hooked me."

"Whatever you say." How she wished she could believe him. She took the opened bottle from him and poured some into the wineglass already on the table.

Before he could respond to her remark, the timer

sounded. "The entrées are ready," she said. "If you'll resume your seat, I'll continue to serve."

"Deal."

Fran took the food from the oven. She arranged it on two plates resting on a warming tray. Then she slipped on pot holders before she went back around the bar and set the servings on the table in front of him.

With one gloved hand she indicated the first plate. "This is veal parmigiana." Pointing to the other, she said, "Stuffed chicken breast with mushrooms and vegetables. Enjoy your meal."

Anxiously, she stood over him and watched while he picked up the fork and sampled everything on each plate. He took a sip of wine, and continued to eat. After finishing the veal, he tasted the chicken again and nodded. Hesitantly, he cut through the green vegetable with his fork and scooped up a small taste. The serious expression on his face told her nothing useful. Curiosity killed the cat and it was about to snuff her, too. Finally, she couldn't stand it any longer.

"Well?" she asked, struggling for nonchalance. "What do you think? How do you like it?"

"Are you fishing for a compliment?" His mouth twitched slightly.

"I want your honest opinion. An objective, yet sincere critique of my work."

"I have to make sure." He took several more bites. "If I'm going to be honest, fair, yet sincere, I need to sample enough product." He scooped up another mouthful.

"Well?" she asked again.

"Just a little more." He picked up his knife, sliced off a bite of the stuffed chicken breast and popped it into his mouth.

"Do you have enough data yet?" she demanded wryly.

"No." He finished off the vegetable and dove into the chicken.

When there were only a couple bites remaining, he put his utensils down and took another sip of wine. "You want my straightforward, unreserved opinion?"

"Don't torture me, Alex."

"Do you really believe I would do that?" His brown eyes sparkled with humor.

"I don't want to believe it. But the evidence is mounting. What do you think?"

"I think it's good."

Her heart fell. "Good? You hate it, don't you?"

"I said it's good." He lifted his gaze to hers. "You want me to embellish?"

She nodded vigorously. "Elaborate, exaggerate, enhance. Adjectives, on the double. And the more the better. But only if you liked it."

"This is, without a doubt, one of the best meals I've ever had." He grinned. "I liked everything, including the vegetable. I suspect a conspiracy. Rosie told you, didn't she?"

"I put in a call to her to stack the deck in my favor. Brussels sprouts was showing off," she said, unable to suppress her smile. "Because to quote your sister, quoting you, I wouldn't eat Brussels sprouts if Wolfgang Puck teamed with Julia Child and won every cooking award from here to New York."

"Well, I guess I have egg on my face."

No, she wanted to say. Just a lovely masculine five o'clock shadow. To cover her reaction, she said, "I did them with honey mustard, mustard seeds lightly toasted, and vinaigrette. They were boiled with the lid off the pot for the best color, I might add." She was babbling and couldn't seem to stop. She *was* nervous, but she also wanted to impress him with her knowledge. "Nutritional analysis—sixty-eight calories, three grams of fat, ten grams of carbohydrates, two grams of protein, no cholesterol, seventy-five milligrams of sodium, thirty percent of calories from fat."

"Carbohydrates? Who knew Brussels sprouts had that?"

"I did."

"Who knew they could taste so good?" he asked.

"I did."

"I guess I owe my sister an apology."

"What did you do to Rosie?"

"I scoffed. She told me that Frannie Carlino—"

Fran shook her head. "She called me Frannie?"

"Yes."

"She knows how I hate that name. I'm going to have to have a talk with your sister."

"Me first. I've got to eat crow, then humble pie, with a generous helping of I-told-you-so for good measure."

"Why?"

"She said she had the right woman for me. She said you could make Brussels sprouts taste good and she was right. I would be a fool to lose you. I'd like to offer—"

"Wait." She held up her hand. "You haven't had dessert."

"Fran," he groaned. "I don't think I could eat another bite. You've convinced me. You know your way around a spice rack. Let's discuss—"

"Tiramisu." She lifted one eyebrow.

"That's not fair," he groaned.

"All's fair in love and war." She shrugged. "Thank

Rosie. She told me tiramisu would be the icing on your cake, so to speak."

He sighed deeply. "The temptations just keep on coming."

My sentiments exactly, she thought, noting his broad chest and wide shoulders, which did his white cotton shirt proud. If this were a date, they would probably move to the couch in front of the TV. The next course would be exploratory kisses that would escalate to passionate and demanding. Then, in an apartment as small as hers, it was only a hop, skip and a jump to the bedroom. If Alex decided to focus his considerable charm and attention on her, Fran wasn't certain she'd have the willpower to put on the brakes.

She had no reason to think he would do that. He'd given her no indication that he even found her attractive. But she felt enough attraction for both of them. And it brought out a peppering of caution. Damn the jerk who had used her and destroyed her trust. But it had happened, and now she couldn't bring herself to ignore the warning signals.

Fran was fairly certain that Alex had been about to offer her the job. She was this close to what she had worked so hard to achieve. But she couldn't ignore her reservations about a close working relationship with him. She had hoped her acute attraction to him was a fluke. This was the third time she'd seen him and it most definitely was not the charm. She wanted the job, but she was afraid her feelings would interfere. All she had to do was figure out a way to broach the subject diplomatically.

"No meal is complete without dessert. Afterward, we can talk business." She watched while he digested her suggestion.

He nodded slowly. "On one condition."

How she hated conditions. Why couldn't he just do it her way? "What?" she asked.

"That you fix yourself a plate and sit down and relax."

"I am relaxed," she said defensively.

He laughed. "Yeah. And I play ukulele for the Los Angeles Philharmonic."

"I sense that you don't believe me."

"It wasn't a criticism, Fran. Just an observation. I'd be skeptical if you weren't nervous. You said yourself that this is a job interview."

"Yes, but—"

"We can put off business talk. Or you can fix yourself a plate. I'll have dessert. And we can discuss your reservations while we eat."

"This isn't negotiable?" she asked.

"Only whether or not you pick up your fork before you listen to my offer." One corner of his mouth lifted in a lazy grin. "I don't want to be accused of being the boss from hell."

"Not likely," she muttered.

"What?"

"Not like me to pass up food," she amended. "A moment on the lips, forever on the hips. A digital scale should be a staple in every chef's kitchen."

"There's nothing wrong with your figure," he commented.

"Thank you." It was hardly even a compliment, but he'd put a smile in her heart.

As she lifted a plate from the cupboard, she mentally threw flame retardant chemicals on the internal glow his words produced. Had he really noticed her shape? Did he like what he saw? Was she his type? Did he have a type? She struggled to put away her curiosity as she took small portions of each entrée and salad that she'd prepared. Then she placed his dessert in front of him. Finally, she took her food and sat down across the table. Suddenly, the forty-two inch diameter didn't seem nearly wide enough.

She took a bite or two before realizing that she was starved. She'd been running on nerves all day in preparation for this interview, and hadn't had the time or inclination to eat much. Everything tasted good.

"Now then," he started. "What's wrong?"

Fran didn't pretend to misunderstand. She hadn't been acting like herself. She owed him an explanation, or at least as much of one as she could give him without making a complete fool of herself.

"Before I answer that question, I think turnabout is fair play. You got to ask me something personal."

"I did? When? What?"

"At dinner last night. You asked me to explain the remark I'd made about taking care of myself. And I said that I'm trying to live my life on my terms and not the ones my family sets."

"I remember." He took a bite of dessert and nodded appreciatively. "This is good enough to eat."

She laughed. "Praise like that could turn my head." She moved the food around her plate without taking a bite. "I'd like to ask you something."

"Okay. Fair is fair."

"Why are you *not* looking for a woman?"

He put his fork down, his carefree demeanor vanishing. His expression turned dark and he looked pained. "I suppose it's pointless to do a ten-minute monologue on why it's perfectly acceptable to be a confirmed bachelor. There doesn't have to be a reason, et cetera."

"I agree." He didn't play games. How refreshing was that?

"I fell in love in college."

"I hear a 'but.' And I have one for you—but I can't believe any woman in her right mind would dump you."

"She didn't," he said sadly. "Her name was Beth and she died."

"Oh, Alex." Fran wished the earth would swallow her whole, right then and there. When would she learn to keep her mouth shut? "I'm so sorry."

Ignoring her consoling words, he continued. "It's very simple, really. Everyone gets a single shot at love, and I had mine. I'm perfectly content with being alone. There's no point in looking for anyone."

She nodded. "I appreciate the clarification."

Fran found his pronouncement profoundly sad. And she hated being proved right about his story having an unhappy ending. Still, it put her at ease with him. She wasn't looking and neither was he, which she found vaguely disappointing. But things got weird when co-workers cozied up. Now she had a guarantee that the work environment would be safe. That left the oven door open to cook up something special—professionally speaking.

"I think it's time to talk business now." She put her fork down and leaned forward eagerly. "So, do I get the nod? The assignment? The job?"

"I'd like to offer you a three-month contract with Marchetti's Inc. At the end of that time, if either party is dissatisfied, we can terminate the association. If not, we can renegotiate. Assuming there's still work to be done." He looked at her. "It's not love or war, but do you think it's fair?"

"I do."

Because it wasn't love and never could be. He'd made that quite clear. So in spite of her attraction, accepting his offer was perfectly safe.

Chapter Four

"You do?" Alex watched Fran nod.

His reply to her question about his love life had obviously allayed whatever misgivings she'd had. The sparkle was back in her eyes.

And he felt as if he was skydiving without a chute. He almost wished this interview had been a disaster. Although it would seriously upset his timetable for the project, he could search for a chef who didn't make him think about soul-stirring kisses instead of stirring marinara sauce. But he would be lying to himself if he said her cooking wasn't among the best he'd ever had.

"Welcome to Marchetti's," he said to Fran. "I'll have the company attorney draw up the contract. You'll receive a call tomorrow for a signature." He held out his hand. "So it's official. You are the new chef for Marchetti's frozen foods—for a minimum of three months and subject to family approval. Let's shake on the deal. Gentleman's agreement."

The way her breasts filled out her hunter-green

sweater put the lie to that statement. As well as the gold hoop earrings dangling daintily from earlobes that he wanted to examine with the tip of his tongue. There was nothing remotely gentlemanly about Fran Carlino. She was all-woman. And he was still free-falling.

She huffed out a breath and the movement did some interesting, downright mouthwatering things to her bosom beneath that sweater. But his brain cleared slightly and he focused enough to realize that something he'd said had put a kink in her wire whisk.

"What?" he asked, dropping his hand.

"You never said anything about family approval."

"It's a family business. I value input from my brothers. The more critical evaluation we can withstand, the better. But I suppose it's normal to be nervous."

"Who said I was nervous?"

"Afraid then."

"I'm not afraid," she said defensively. "You just never mentioned that the recipes I develop will be subject to a family thumbs-up."

"We're not known as the meddling Marchettis for nothing. And anyone who cooks like you has nothing to worry about." Her shoulders relaxed. "Then we have a deal?" He held out his hand again.

She hesitated two beats before reaching across the table to put her small hand in his. "Done," she said, then resumed eating.

Alex breathed a sigh of relief. All hurdles successfully cleared. But he couldn't help wondering why it had been so important for her to know the reason he wasn't actively dating. His answer had obviously swung her pendulum in the direction of an affirmative answer to his job offer. But his curiosity got the better of him.

"Tell me, Fran, if I had said I was single, available and eagerly looking for someone, would you still have accepted the job?"

She chewed thoughtfully for several moments. "My answer would have been the same."

"But?" he prompted.

One corner of her full mouth lifted wryly. "I'm not sure how you knew there was a 'but,' but you're right. I need the job. That's not a national secret. And thank you very much for the offer. *But* I would have been on pins and needles."

"Why?"

"Waiting for you to hit on me." She looked taken aback for a moment, as if she couldn't believe she'd said that out loud. "Not that you would," she amended. "You've been very professional and I'd expect nothing less. But the possibility could have existed, and I'd have been tense, waiting for the world's cleverest pickup line."

"Like 'what's your sign?'" he asked wryly.

"That's ancient history. You really are out of practice."

"So what is the current come-on dialogue?"

She thought for a minute. "I can't even tell you. It's been a while for me, too." Her forehead puckered slightly and her cocoa-colored eyes narrowed, as if she was remembering something unpleasant.

Why? A woman as attractive, lively and sexy as Fran Carlino should have men waiting in line. Yet not only was that not the case, he wasn't convinced that she would have taken the job if he'd told her he was available. He had a feeling her wariness was more than just not wanting to follow in her mother's footsteps with a husband and family. What had happened to make her gun-shy?

This was none of his business. Their acquaintance had progressed to employment. That didn't give him the right to her life history. In fact, the less he knew the better. And his parachute had just opened, he realized. Neither he nor Fran was interested in anything personal. There was safety in numbers, or at least in being on the same page in the cookbook.

"Well, I couldn't be more delighted that you accepted my offer," he said, meaning every word. "You're the right choice for the position. I'm looking forward to seeing what you cook up in the corporate kitchen."

"Me, too." She held up her wineglass. "Here's to a successful business association."

She took a sip of her wine, then tucked a wayward strand of brown hair behind her ear. The glare from the light over her table put a glisten on the moisture clinging to her top lip. He suddenly had an almost overwhelming urge to kiss it away, to know if her mouth was as soft and exciting as it looked.

"I didn't know you'd been married," she said out of the blue.

The sudden stab of discomfort from her remark almost distracted him enough to keep him from noticing that she'd turned the conversation away from herself and their professional connection, back to him.

"I wasn't married," he answered.

"But I thought... You said..." She stopped.

"I said I fell in love. Beth and I never married."

He pulled in a deep breath in spite of the guilt and pain that settled in his chest—two old friends that he'd learned to live with.

"Why not?" Fran asked softly, her brown eyes filled with sympathy.

"This from a woman who thinks marriage is equivalent to serfdom."

She looked sheepish. "But I'm not the average woman."

"You'll get no argument from me about that."

"Did you just pay me a compliment or cut me off at the knees?"

He folded his napkin and set it on the table before leaning back in his chair. "I was merely stating a fact."

"So why didn't you tie the knot with Beth?"

"I wanted to wait until my career with the company was well established before taking that step. He who hesitates is lost," he added softly, hoping he'd successfully sifted the bitterness from his tone.

"So you wish you had?"

He nodded. "More than anything, Beth wanted to be a wife, mother, homemaker. I could have given that to her for what little time we would have had. But I thought other things were more important."

"Hindsight is twenty-twenty," she said. "Maybe you weren't sure? About being in love?"

He shook his head. "I was sure. Just short-sighted," he said, pushing his glasses up more firmly on his nose. Her fleeting smile at his pun tugged at his heart. "I thought I was being noble. When we married, I wanted to be able to devote more attention to her, our relationship and establishing a home than my job. As it turned out, that's all I have now."

"Seems to me your niche in the business was assured. Even the third son isn't going to get canned if there's a spot for him."

"What does that mean?"

"Nothing. Just that I can understand channeling energy into your career if you've just been hired by a company. Heaven knows I plan to give it my best shot. In case you were wondering. But you were groomed from childhood for the family business. Your position was secure. You and Beth could have married."

"Don't you think I've told myself that a million times?" He didn't even try to suppress his bitterness. "Maybe I'd have a child now. A part of her still with me." His voice rose a notch.

"I'm sorry." Fran shook her head. "There I go, getting myself into trouble with my mouth again. I'd be better off putting food in it instead of my foot."

He could think of a much better way to keep her mouth out of trouble. The idea flashed into his mind, and he felt even more disloyal to Beth's memory. "Forget it."

"I'll try. But first I've got one more question."

Somehow he knew she would ask it no matter what he said.

"Okay. One more," he agreed, bracing himself.

"Why are you so convinced that you get only one shot at love?"

"Heredity."

"There's a Marchetti gene for being a one-woman man?" she asked.

"Or a one-man woman. Rosie fell in love with her husband, Steve, when they were just kids. He'd been abandoned at a bus station by his mother and was being raised by his grandmother. Nick took him under his wing, and Steve was sort of unofficially adopted by the family. Rosie believed in him when he didn't believe in himself.

"And you can blame my father for us confirmed bachelors," Alex added.

"I'm not sure *blame* is the right word. But why your father?"

"He's been chasing my mother around the kitchen— that's just a figure of speech. Don't read anything into it on the gene scale, or because you'll be working in *my* kitchen," he clarified at her narrow-eyed look. "Let me rephrase. They've been together for thirty-five years."

"That's pretty special in this day and age," she agreed.

He nodded. "My brother Joe hinted that they'd had problems at one point when we were small. They separated for a short time. But Tom Marchetti loves Flo— for better or worse."

"What about your brothers? Abby is obviously a happy woman with your brother Nick."

"He gave her a job in one of the restaurants when she was just eighteen years old and she'd lost her parents in an auto accident."

"That's awful," Fran said. "I mean about her parents, not the job."

"It took them a long time to get together, but one look at Abby and there was no one else for Nick. He was even secretly married for a short time, before that. When he opened a restaurant in Phoenix, a pregnant waitress was dumped by her boyfriend and Nick thought he loved her and wanted a family."

"What happened?"

"The boyfriend had a change of heart and she had the marriage to Nick annulled. That made him gun-shy. But true love won out for him and Abby."

"What about Joe? Isn't he the one getting married on Valentine's Day?"

Alex grinned. "You're good."

"I've had training in keeping track of large numbers of brothers. It's the Carlino curse."

He chuckled. "Joe met his fiancée in the hospital when Rosie gave birth. Nurse Liz got his attention when she dragged him out of my sister's room by his ear. He tried to charm her into letting him stay after visiting hours were over. Up until then, he was pretty vocal about his confirmed bachelor status. They had some things to work through, but once he saw her it was all over but the shouting."

"Which will happen at the wedding."

"That's the plan. Luke and I are the last bachelors."

"So how does a confirmed bachelor like yourself fill his time?"

"Work. It saved me after Beth died." He took in a big breath and waited for the pain to hit. Vaguely surprised when it was dull to nonexistent, he continued. "The family business kept me from giving her the family she wanted, but it was also my salvation."

He'd buried himself in work to get through every day without Beth. One day turned into another, then another until somehow the years had passed. He liked what he did for a living and was grateful to have it. But he'd just told Fran about his siblings pairing off and their personal happiness. He felt left behind, lonely and vaguely discontented.

"I'm sorry. Me and my big mouth again. Feel free to tell me to mind my own business."

"It's not painful." And to his shock, he realized that was true.

"So you're past the pain of losing Beth, and you really do believe that we only get one shot at love?"

"I do."

"Then what's your excuse? For working so hard now, I mean?"

"You said it yourself. Second-son syndrome."

"I was teasing."

He toyed with the fork on his dessert plate. "Maybe. But you made me realize something."

"Wow. Maybe I should hang out my shingle for family counseling."

"No way. For someone who knows her way around herbs and spices the way you do, it would be a crime."

"Thank you. But don't for a minute believe a compliment will distract me from ferreting out information. What did you realize?" she asked.

"That a man needs goals. The business is doing extremely well, thanks to my brothers. None of us has to wonder where our next meal is coming from. But I want to make my mark in the company. I'm working for the satisfaction of a job well done. I want this line of frozen cuisine to be an unqualified success."

"I still think you're using frozen foods to warm your bed at night." She smiled at her metaphoric contradiction.

"That's not what this is about. And I thought we agreed no more armchair psychology."

"Sorry. I forgot."

"I'm beginning to see that it's a habit of yours to forget when you have every intention of speaking your mind." He stood up. "Before you get on a roll, I think it's time for me to go."

She stood also and followed him to the door. "So when do you want me to start?"

"When are you available?"

"Now. My contract is up. The loose ends are essentially tied up. I can give two weeks' notice. That will make it politically correct.''

"How about two weeks, then? Which will be the middle of December. Do you mind starting before Christmas? We could push back the starting date to the first of the year if—''

She shook her head. ''The sooner we get going on your project the better. I'm committed to helping you overcome second-son syndrome. Together we can show the rest of the Marchettis that third son does more than twiddle his thumbs in that corner office.'' She smiled as she opened the door.

For several moments, they stared at each other. Alex realized he was strangely reluctant to leave. Partly because he'd enjoyed her company, and partly because he wasn't sure how to say goodbye.

Oh, he knew the word. *Goodbye.* Two syllables. But should he shake her hand? After all, this was business. But it felt cold. So wrong for a woman with Fran's verve, animation and friendliness. Kiss her on the cheek? Warmer. But not his first choice. On the mouth? Bingo. Hot. Boiling, in fact. But inappropriate, not to mention unprofessional. Unfortunately, it was very much what he wanted to do. This was the damnedest job interview he'd ever conducted.

He decided it would be best not to touch her at all.

"Good night, Alex,'' she prompted.

"Good night. I'll see you in two weeks, Frannie.''

He was out the door before she could say "Smile when you call me that.'' But he couldn't help smiling with anticipation.

It just seemed a long time until he would see her again.

* * *

Waiting to start her new job had been the longest two weeks of Fran's life. Although not nearly enough time to forget the timbre of Alex's voice when he'd called her "Frannie." The hated nickname wrapped in seduction had rendered her speechless. And then she couldn't seem to get it out of her mind. Ever since accepting the job, she'd agonized over whether or not she'd made the right decision.

Now it was her first day of work at Marchetti's. Alex had introduced her to his three brothers and given her the tour of the corporate offices. Not once had he used the husky tone that sent shivers through her. But he *had* saved the best for last: the first-floor kitchen used for research and development.

It was large, probably as big as her apartment, with an island work center in the middle. There was a stainless steel refrigerator and a matching freezer, both walk-ins, no less. She glanced inside a well-stocked pantry that would hold her queen-size bed with enough space left to walk around it. The rest of the room had cupboards, lots and lots, covered with countertops tough enough to chop and dice on. There were several ovens and microwaves.

"This is terrific," she said. "And that adjective doesn't do it justice. It's really awesome."

"I'm glad you approve." He pointed to a door on one side. "Through there is the employee lounge."

"Handy."

"We try to think of everything. Even guinea pigs— I mean loyal, committed employees eager to test our latest concoctions."

He grinned and her world tilted until she wanted to grab on to something—preferably him—to steady herself. Alex stood beside her, hands on hips. His red tie was loosened and the long sleeves of his powder blue shirt were rolled up. In navy slacks and black leather loafers, he appeared the successful executive he was.

Her culinary training had taught her to use all her senses—taste, touch, sight, sound and smell. Unfortunately, that training spilled over into the rest of her life, including sensory data regarding Alex. He was good-looking, with a wonderfully rich, deep voice that burrowed inside her and made her stomach quiver. And he smelled so good, a combination of some masculine, spicy aftershave and soap that made her want to snuggle against him. She hadn't touched or tasted him. But with little or no effort she could imagine how it could be akin to a religious experience. Her susceptible heart went pitter-pat.

She didn't know what to say next, and with luck her self-consciousness didn't show. She hoped he would assume that she was impressed, and just looking around the corporate kitchen had rendered her speechless.

"Feel free to explore the cupboards," he offered. "They're loaded with all kinds of gadgets. But you should take inventory and let me know if there's something else you need."

"I'd love to snoop," she agreed. That would give her an excuse to move away from his side without looking like an army in full retreat.

Fran spent the next few minutes opening drawers and cupboard doors, investigating all the nooks and crannies. There was an impressive array of knives in all sizes, a food processor, blender, two graters—hand and electric—peelers, choppers, dicers and slicers. This kitchen had all the bells and whistles she could imagine.

After a hands-on exploration of everything in the

room, with the exception of her boss, she took a deep breath and leaned against the white countertop. "If there's anything missing, I don't see it."

"Good." He pointed to the far side of the room and a built-in desk that matched the birch cabinets. "There's a computer set up. You can keep recipes, records, notes on it if you'd like. I'm not sure how you work and track results. But I would be happy to give you an orientation on the programs if you'd like."

"Great." She nodded with satisfaction. "I take hard copy notes about everything I work on—ingredients, prep time, cook time, level of success based on certain criteria. Nutrients, food value, that sort of thing. Entering the results into the computer is the last thing I do. It keeps me organized. But I like to maintain the scrap paper, too."

He folded his arms over his chest. "Whatever works."

"Okay," she said, nodding with satisfaction. "It's time to talk turkey. Or should I say linguine."

"Translation?" he asked, lifting one dark eyebrow.

"We need to discuss what entrées you want in the launch campaign."

"Right. Let's go back up to my office."

"I'm right behind you, fearless leader."

He shook his head as he led the way to the elevator. "Is it too much to ask that for the duration of our professional collaboration you could give me some respect?"

Fran knew he was kidding. "I thought that's what I just did. Is there another form of address that would work better for you? Like Emperor or Pharaoh, or your exalted highness?"

"Just Alex," he said, shaking his head with a resigned sigh.

"What, no reprimand? If this is the extent of your temperamental ways, I think I can bear up."

They entered the elevator. Just the two of them, alone. It was very private, intimate even, though it was essentially a business setting. No one could hear or see them if they shared a stolen kiss. The thought cranked up Fran's heart rate, and her cheeks felt the heat. He might be able to bear up because he wasn't interested in her. But could she?

Memories of cooking school washed over her. Colin coaxing her into dark corners for stolen kisses, places where they could have been discovered. The excitement of it all. Followed by the worst humiliation, betrayal and pain she'd ever known. An experience she'd vowed never to repeat. She could chalk up her unfortunate error in judgment to youth and inexperience. But she was older and wiser now. She would be a fool to let this attraction for Alex continue. He was her boss, for goodness' sake.

Say something, she ordered herself. Anything to distract her from her far too hunky employer.

"Okay, just Alex, tell me about your ideas for the entrées," she said. "The sooner I know what you want, the sooner I can start the ingredients percolating in my mind. You've heard the expression 'look before you leap'?"

"I believe I have heard that somewhere," he said, his mouth turning up at the corners.

"I can't just step into that state-of-the-art kitchen and start throwing stuff together," she informed him. "If I think about it ahead of time, the process goes much faster."

''That makes sense,'' he agreed. ''I've actually done my own version of 'look before you leap'. I want to compete in the food service market on several levels. The harried working woman, the single guy who wants to impress the woman in his life.''

''What about the single gal looking to snag her bachelor and drag him back to her cave?'' she asked, trying to look serious and failing miserably when he grinned. ''I'm sure you've heard of a little thing called women's liberation?''

''That works, too,'' he said. ''Either way, I want to overlap the market as much as possible.''

''So what have you come up with?''

The elevator doors opened, and he held out his hand for her to precede him. ''After you,'' he said.

She breathed a sigh of relief as she left the car. Never again would she be able to think of an elevator in quite the same utilitarian way. She had chattered like a moronic magpie to keep her mind off how exciting it would be to kiss Alex there. She hoped that, for the duration of this assignment, she never again would have to share such a small space, or even a large space, with him unchaperoned.

They walked side by side down the carpeted hall to his office. His secretary was seated at her post, with every hair of her cap of gray curls in place.

She smiled in a friendly, maternal way. ''Nice to see you again, Miss Carlino.''

''You remember me,'' Fran answered.

''I do indeed. Alex made it impossible to forget you,'' she said, eyes twinkling.

''Really?'' Fran stared at him. ''How?''

''She's exaggerating.'' Alex looked decidedly uncomfortable. ''This is Joyce Barnes.''

"It's a pleasure to meet you, Joyce," Fran said, shaking the other woman's hand.

"Same here." Then she said to Alex, "Nick called. I left the message on your desk."

"Thank you, Joyce. Please hold my calls. I have business to discuss with Fran and I don't want to be interrupted unless someone's bleeding or on fire."

"Yes, sir," his secretary said.

They went into his office and he closed the door. Then he sat down behind his desk while Fran took one of the chairs facing it.

"Okay. Now." He took a folder and opened it. "I've done some research into consumption trends. Pizza is the one entrée that far and away consistently charts as the top seller."

"That doesn't surprise me." She couldn't help thinking how cute he looked when he put on his intense and earnest expression. Or how appealing his discomfort when his secretary had let slip that he'd made it impossible to forget her. "Go on," she encouraged.

"Frozen pizza currently accounts for approximately seven point two percent of the twenty-five-billion-dollar-market of total pizza sales. Since 1989, the volume of frozen pizza purchased per household has shown consistent gains."

"Fascinating," she said, looking at his mouth. There was a sensuality about his lips, and the idea made her tingle all over. "Tell me more."

"I want kids."

"I beg your pardon?"

"The kids market," he clarified, looking up from his notes to meet her gaze. "It's heating up the pizza arena. A study shows that more than half the kids under thirteen surveyed said that pizza is their favorite food. And close to sixty-five percent of American kids today are preparing at least one meal a week by themselves.''

"And you want it to be a Marchetti's pizza."

"Yes." He rested his elbows on his desk and leaned forward intensely. "It's got to be microwavable and oven friendly."

"Since when are culinary and computer terminology interchangeable?" she asked, her mouth twitching.

"You know what I mean," he said.

"I do. Sorry. And not a problem. I can adapt the pizza recipe for nuking. What else is on your list?"

"Spaghetti and meatballs. That's a restaurant favorite and easy to freeze."

Fran met his gaze. "So when did you graduate from culinary school?" she asked sweetly.

"It was the school of hard knocks, and my father was headmaster. My brothers and I all worked in various capacities, including cook, in the restaurant while we were in high school and college."

"I see. And you're right. Adjusting that is a piece of cake. Please go on."

"Lasagna's a given."

"Agreed."

He handed her a sheet of paper. "And I'd like you to incorporate this recipe."

She took the sheet and carefully looked it over, her stomach knotting. "Now we've got a problem."

Chapter Five

"I don't want to hear the words *problem* or *trouble*," he said, only half kidding.

Up until a second ago, Alex had been enjoying his job more than he ever had. He'd anticipated Fran's first day from the moment she'd signed the contract the legal department had messengered over to her. He'd taken enormous satisfaction from her pleasure in the corporate kitchen, as if he'd given her a particularly expensive piece of jewelry to impress her. Life was good. Until he heard the word *problem*.

"Okay. What?" he asked, leaning forward to rest his forearms on his desk.

"This recipe calls for fresh ricotta."

He nodded. "I'm aware of that."

She shifted uncomfortably in her chair. "It doesn't freeze well."

"You mean in freezing temperatures it won't harden?"

She sighed. "I mean after that, when it thaws out.

Nine times out of ten it's too grainy and watery to use in uncooked recipes, like cannoli filling.''

"But this is stuffed shells," he pointed out. "They get cooked."

"I'm aware of that," she said, repeating his words.

"There's ricotta in lasagna. It gets baked. You gave that one the go-ahead."

"In lasagna, where you've got mozzarella and sauce to camouflage its unpleasant texture, it's not a problem. But shells are right out there. I think you should look for something else."

"This is a signature dish at all the Marchetti's Restaurants." And one of his personal favorites.

"Surely there's another one you could substitute. I thought you wanted the launch campaign to be a success."

"I do. And this is one of our most popular entrées."

"I'm not sure I can make it work," she said, shaking her head as she looked over the recipe again.

"It's your job to make it work," he pointed out.

Her chin lifted in a subtly defiant, defensive movement. "And what if I can't?"

"I have faith in your expertise."

"I'm good, but even the best chef is limited by the characteristics of her ingredients. I'll attempt this if you insist, but I think it's a losing proposition. If failure is not an option, maybe it would be best if we terminate our contract now. I know the project means a lot to you and I don't want to waste your time."

That would mean not seeing her—at work, he amended. Or having the benefit of her experience and imagination involved in the project. And *that* was not an option. Again, he couldn't help thinking that something had happened to make her defensive. He wished he knew what it was. He couldn't let her get away. Her absence would put a crimp in his heart—or rather, the project that was dear to his heart.

His jaw tightened as he shook his head. "If I'm wrong, I'll accept responsibility."

She murmured something that sounded a lot like "I'll believe that when a pregnant ape swings across the room." But he decided to let it pass.

"Okay, I'll give it a shot," she agreed. "And if I'm wrong, you can have my resignation instead."

A month later, Fran was still stewing about her conversation with Alex. He had never said he wouldn't accept her resignation. Anger and frustration sifted through her as she looked at the watery, unattractive mess she'd made of the recipe he'd given her. She'd tried everything she could think of to adapt it and make it a winner. But if the cook gave it two thumbs down, what would Alex's family say? The Carlino boys were pretty vocal when it came to food. Since it was their livelihood, she expected the Marchettis would be even more outspoken.

"Two more months on my blasted contract," she muttered, tossing a wooden spoon into the sink. Marinara sauce splattered the white countertop. "This is just a means to an end, a restaurant of my own. Then I call the shots. After that, I don't have to put up with him. He's just like all the rest."

"Who's just like all the rest?" a female voice asked from behind her.

She whirled to see Rosie Schafer leaning her elbows on the center island work area. "You startled me," Fran blurted out, resting a palm against her pounding heart. "I didn't hear you come in."

"You were too busy talking to yourself."

Fran grabbed a dish rag and mopped up the red streaks. "I wish you hadn't seen that."

"Who did you really want to wallop with that wooden spoon?"

"I'm not sure it would be politically correct to confide that information," Fran said cautiously.

Rosie nodded knowingly. "What did Alex do?"

"What makes you think he did something?" she hedged, meeting the other woman's gaze with the island between them.

"I figured it had to be one of my brothers. You don't have to answer directly to Nick, Joe or Luke. By process of elimination it has to be Alex. So what did he do?"

"Since my present employment is precarious anyway, I suppose there's no harm in telling my boss's sister." She leaned her elbows on the countertop and rested her chin in her hands, then let out a long, discouraged breath. "He insisted a certain recipe be included in the frozen food campaign. I'm having trouble with it."

"Hmm."

"I don't like the sound of that." Fran straightened. "What does that mean?"

"I've been notified of a family tasting to try out the new frozen entrées."

Fran groaned. "Yeah, it's coming up a week from today. I've got everything ready for the other dishes. But this one..." She shook her head. "I'm afraid my days with Marchetti's are numbered. I'm prepared to bow out gracefully."

"Why would you think Alex would let you go over this?" Rosie asked. "By definition, research and development means trial and error. If it doesn't work, you go to plan B.''

"He said if it doesn't work he would take responsibility.''

"Silly me. You're right, of course. Them's fightin' words. That sounds like a man who plans to fire you if you burn the food. He might even lop off your head for good measure.''

Fran realized that Rosie had no basis for understanding. She didn't work in the restaurant business with her brothers. In fact, she'd opted to open her own bookstore instead. She couldn't possibly comprehend the pressure and prejudice Fran constantly faced.

"Go ahead. Joke about it. But the food service industry doesn't look kindly on women. It's every man for himself. And I do mean man. Maybe I should have listened to my father and become a housewife. My career path doesn't pander to the faint of heart. This industry is survival of the fittest.''

"And that's different from being a wife and mother how?'' Rosie asked good-naturedly.

"Sorry. I meant no disrespect for the important job you do, in addition to running your own bookstore. It's just… I learned early on that men in charge are only too willing to believe the worst about a woman in this business. I had a bad experience and it showed me how cutthroat this life is. Alex lulled me into a false sense of security. I guess I'm lucky that he showed his true colors right away. He's just like every other man.''

"What man took a bite out of you?'' Rosie asked sympathetically.

Fran laughed, but there was no humor in it. "Trust me. You don't want to know the long, sad, but essentially boring story. And I'm not anxious to share the memories of my young and foolish days. Suffice it to say I'm sadder, but wiser now.''

"Okay. You don't have to talk about it if you don't want to. But you can trust me on this. Alex is different. He won't hang you out to dry at the tasting just to cover his own behind.''

"I have a hard time believing he's different.''

"Just wait. He'll prove it to you. At least let him mess up before you get mad." Her face took on an "aha" expression. "I get the feeling you want him to fire you.''

"That's silly," Fran answered with a tad too much bluster.

"What are you really afraid of, Fran?''

"I'm terrified that these shells are going to crash and burn. Or should I say capsize and sink?''

"I don't really need to know, but don't lie to yourself." Rosie gazed at her sympathetically. "Here's food for thought…''

"Nice pun," Fran said grinning.

"Thanks. I love it when that happens. But seriously, there's something you and Alex have in common. You've both been hurt.''

Maybe. But it was incredibly unprofessional of Fran to discuss him with his sister. "I'm really nervous about unveiling the entrées," she admitted, changing the subject.

"Don't be. It's just the family. You'll love them.''

"I've already met upper management—Nick, Joe and Luke. They seem nice.''

"They are. But don't ever tell them I said that.'' Rosie grinned as she tucked a wayward strand of dark, curly hair behind her ear. "Besides, I don't think the whole family will be able to make it.''

"Oh? Who's not coming?" Fran asked.

"Me and Steve. Abby. Liz."

"So who *is* going to be there?"

"Nick, Joe, and Alex, of course. Luke and Mom and Dad."

"Ah," Fran said. "Just everyone who gets a vote."

"Stop worrying, Fran." Rosie sniffed. "There's something divinely aromatic in the air. If it tastes as good as my sniffer says, you've got it made in the shade. The Marchetti brothers will make you their queen. The family is going to love you."

"I just want them to love my cooking," she countered.

But she wondered if that was entirely true. Even though she was annoyed with Alex, she wanted to impress him. And it bugged her no end that she didn't just mean here at work, in the frozen food department. What fried her most was that she couldn't seem to shake the *need* for his approval of her as a woman.

In addition to shaking her professional image, had the jerk from school destroyed her confidence in her femininity? Fran tried to tell herself no, but what other explanation could there be? Because come hell or high water, she would not let herself succumb to any real or imagined temptation for a man in the food service business who also happened to be her employer.

Fran looked at the other woman and sighed. "I'm pretty sure the concoction you smell is going to melt in one's proverbial mouth. There's only one major problem."

"And that is?"

"It's my recipe, not one of the ones that Alex gave me to adapt."

Rosie frowned. "I don't know what prejudice

you've experienced in the business, Fran. And no one knows better than me that the Marchetti men have their faults. But no one can accuse them of being stupid.''

"And by that you mean?"

"If your recipe is as good as you say, and as good as I think, you'll get to showcase it."

"Time will tell." Fran shook her head to clear it, then looked at her friend. "It just occurred to me to wonder what you're doing here. Don't you have a business to run?"

Rosie nodded. "I left Jackie in charge for a little while."

"Did you come by to check up on one of your brothers?"

"In a manner of speaking." Rosie shrugged. "I was just wondering how you and Alex are getting along."

"I guess my tirade answered that question loud and clear. 'Nuff said.''

"Yes." Rosie nodded, smiling enthusiastically. "You two are right on schedule."

"Actually, we're ahead of schedule. The test tasting wasn't supposed to happen for another four to six weeks," Fran clarified.

"That's not what I meant. I knew you were the perfect woman for him. And I was referring to the romantic agenda."

"You're not still matchmaking!" Fran accused. She put her hands on her hips and glared at Alex's sister.

"Still? You mean he saw through me?" she asked, dark eyes twinkling.

"Like clear-paned glass. He told me so the first night he came to my apartment, using the flimsy excuse of returning the baby food jars."

"He's smarter than I thought."

Fran could have told her that. But she wanted to know more about the "schedule." "What did you mean about Alex and me being right on schedule?"

"You wanted to brain him. Passionately," she added, raising one dark eyebrow suggestively.

Fran shook her head so hard that her hair loosened and fell, tumbling around her shoulders. She pulled out the clip. "That's not funny, Rosie. There is nothing of a personal nature between Alex and me. For goodness' sake, you saw me talking to myself when you walked in. About him," she added.

"I know," Rosie said, nodding enthusiastically. "It's a sure sign that things are progressing nicely. You always want to clobber them before you kiss them."

"The thought of kissing your brother has never entered my mind," she said, crossing her fingers behind her back to nullify the lie.

"Methinks she doth protest too much." Rosie held up her hand. "Never mind. Forget I said anything. It's enough that I know the seed is planted and starting to sprout. Time will tell if my efforts bear fruit."

Fran feigned a sympathetic look as she patted the other woman's hand. "I'm glad you came to see me, Mother Earth. You need to get out of the bookstore more often. In fact, you need to branch out from the romance section to mysteries. I can tell from this nonsense about Alex and me that you've already been dabbling in science fiction."

"Very funny, Fran."

"I hate to say you're wrong, but when the shoe fits…" She shrugged. "I'm not the perfect woman, not for any man. And especially not for Alex. He told me about Beth." She couldn't help asking, "What was she like?"

Rosie hesitated several moments before saying, "She was a good person and very solicitous of Alex."

Fran nodded knowingly. "So he had his shot at love. He'll never feel that way again."

"Time will tell," Rosie said as she walked to the doorway. She grinned wickedly. "I still believe I'm right. And when you and Alex wind up together, I can say I told you so. Only I won't. Not only am I above that, I'll be too overjoyed to finally see my brother happy."

Before she could retort, Rosie was gone. Fran had to admit Alex was tempting. She'd worked with him a month now, and instead of waning, her attraction was more acute. She smiled, recalling the first time they'd talked. She had to admit Alex looked twice as cute as when she had first laid eyes on him. And the glow he'd put in her heart then now threatened to erupt into a full-blown fire. The only thing that had saved her from herself was his disinterest. He'd made no move, given her no indication that he found her the least bit attractive.

And she was relieved, she told herself. With time, effort, several cold showers a day and a stroll into the walk-in freezer, she might even convince herself of that. But it was for the best that he wasn't interested in her. Not only was she philosophically opposed to being anyone's wife, she didn't believe the man existed who could change her mind about marriage. Even if she found a man she could trust to tell her the truth. A man she could believe loved her for herself. Even then, a walk down the aisle was not for her.

She just hoped Rosie wasn't disappointed two months from now when her contract expired and the matchmaking was a dismal failure.

* * *

Alex walked into the corporate kitchen to make sure everything was ready for Operation Third Son. He smiled at the thought, remembering Fran's analysis of his motivation. It was fish or cut bait time. The family was due any minute. He didn't see Fran, but the freezer door was open.

"Hello? Anyone home?" he called out.

Fran walked out, followed by a cold mist. She was all in white—pants, a long-sleeved cotton shirt, topped off with a spotless apron. She smiled a welcome, and he couldn't help thinking that she exuded enough warmth to melt everything in the deep freeze. Including his heart. He shook his head, banishing that thought and the guilt that followed.

"Hi," he said, shoving his hands in his pockets. "Is everything ready?"

She nodded. "The entrées are frozen. When your family gets here, I'll microwave them for everyone to taste." She let out a long, steadying breath.

"You're not nervous, are you?" he asked.

"Me?" she said brightly. "Only about everything."

"Define 'everything.'"

"The entrées. Not letting you down. Spending time with the royal Marchetti hierarchy." She made a dismissive gesture with her hand. "Piece of cake."

"You already know Nick, Joe and Luke. Ma and Dad are going to love you."

"Rosie said the same thing when she stopped by last week."

"What else did she say?" he asked.

"Idle chitchat," Fran answered vaguely, not meeting his gaze.

Translation: matchmaking. He knew Rosie. When

she got an idea in her head, especially about romance, she didn't let it go without a fight. She took after their mother. But he didn't want to go there any more than Fran did.

"Okay," he said briskly. "Do you mind if I take a look? At our babies? The entrées," he clarified at her startled expression.

"You're the boss," she said. But her mouth pulled into a straight line. Her body tensed.

Problem? How he hated that word. He knew the stuffed shells were giving her fits, but he crossed his fingers as he walked into the freezer. To his right on the shelf were the frozen main dishes, all lined up. He saw pizza, spaghetti and meatballs, lasagna, and a good-looking arrangement of stuffed shells and marinara sauce. Then he noticed another dish. It was angel hair pasta with some kind of white sauce. Someone, namely his sexy-as-hell chef, was cooking up rebellion in the ranks.

He walked out and shut the door behind him. "What's with the fifth entrée?" he asked casually.

She squared her shoulders, standing as tall as her five-foot-two status allowed. Then she looked him dead in the eye. "I thought it prudent to have another choice in the wings, just in case."

"I don't know what you're worried about. The shells dish looks great," he protested.

"I agree. But it's still in one solid, appealing piece. Wait till it's nuked."

"You're borrowing trouble."

"You've seen it yourself, Alex," she protested.

He nodded. "I didn't think it was that bad." But he was nervous about it, too. "Let's hold off on the last one until we see how the first four go."

"I'd like to unveil it along with the others. It's a new recipe of mine," she said. "I need the objective feedback. The ingredients are minimal and it's not labor intensive, which would maximize profit. And I think it tastes pretty good. If I do say so myself."

He shook his head, reluctant to present too many choices and confuse the issue. "I still want to hold off."

Her chin rose slightly in the way he was beginning to recognize as defiance. She didn't give up easily. Unlike Beth. The idea popped into his mind. He recalled the way his fiancée had always catered to his wishes. Like waiting on the wedding, he thought. He looked at the obstinate expression in Fran's brown eyes, turning them dark as coals, and couldn't picture her knuckling under if she wanted to get married. Which she'd made it clear she didn't.

He shook his head slightly. No, Fran was nothing like Beth. And that wasn't altogether a bad thing.

"I still want to bring it out tonight." She folded her arms over her chest and stared at him, the walking, talking, breathing definition of stubborn.

They stood there, waiting for the other to blink. "I'm the boss, Fran. And I say we hold off."

"I'm the chef. And I want the feedback."

"Are you going to make me pull rank?"

"Not unless you dismiss my solution to the stalemate."

He put his hands on his hips and stared down at her. "And that would be?"

"We arm wrestle." She met his gaze with a mutinous one of her own. "If you win, I'll put my epicurean triumph aside, albeit reluctantly. If I win, we serve it tonight along with the others, as if we'd planned it that way.''

He couldn't help it. He laughed. "I'm practically twice your size. I outweigh you by eighty pounds.''

"Ninety-five easy," she snapped.

"Whatever. It wouldn't be fair," he objected.

"I thought you were different," she said, shaking her head. "But you're as autocratic as every man I've ever met. More," she added with spirit.

"I'm just trying to be fair. But if you really want to lose, far be it from me to be just and impartial.''

She put her elbow on the corner of the island with her hand raised and fire in her eyes. "Let's do it.''

"You're on. But I want to go on record that I feel a little guilty taking advantage of you.''

"Don't lose any sleep over it," she said, her expression glowing with mischief.

He rested his elbow beside hers. His arm was longer and he had to adjust his position so that he could grasp her small, delicate hand. This went against everything his father had ever taught him about being a gentleman, about looking after a woman, about respecting the weaker sex. Although he had doubts about that last part when he was a bit distracted by her closeness, her feminine scent, the warmth of her small hand in his larger one, the delicacy of her fingers. He shook his head to clear it. There was no possible way he could lose. He had her on size and strength.

"Go," she said, tensing her arm as she tried to push his hand to the counter, without success.

Exhilaration coursed through him and heated his blood. Damn, but his job had spiced up since he'd hired Fran.

"You can use both hands if you'd like," he offered graciously.

"Don't do me any favors."

"Okay. But I don't want to hurt you." He grinned. "Anytime you want to give, just say the word."

"I'd rather eat glass," she said, slightly breathless from her exertion.

"It's your call."

One minute Alex was enjoying himself immensely. He was looking into her snapping brown eyes and thinking how beautiful she was. Her lips were full and soft and so close he would hardly have to move to... The next instant, she leaned closer and put her mouth on his.

His first thought was that she tasted better—felt softer—than he'd ever imagined. His next was that he wanted to stay there forever and explore the depths of her sweetness. Heat raced through his body as his heart rate doubled. Blood pounded in his ears. His breathing quickened when he heard Fran's soft, eminently feminine moan of pleasure.

Unsatisfied by the stiff seam of her lips, he traced it with his tongue, and she instantly opened to him. He explored the moist, honeyed sweetness, enjoying the seductive intimacy. Not to mention the fact that her breathing was fast and furious.

He lifted his free hand and slid his fingers into her hair, releasing the upswept silkiness from the single clip. The strands cascaded around her face, and he cupped his palm to the back of her head, making the contact of their mouths more firm, more secure.

Still it wasn't enough. He tried to pull her into his arms and realized the counter was in the way. Moving back slightly, he saw the flush on her cheeks, the brightness in her eyes, the rapid rise and fall of her chest. He wanted her. What a feeling! Until that moment he hadn't realized how much he'd missed holding a woman, kissing her. Or maybe it was just kissing Fran.

He was about to step around the counter and tug her against him when she shook her head slightly, then pinned his arm to the countertop.

Breathlessly she said, "I win. We're showing my entrée."

Instantly he straightened. "You cheated."

She took a big breath, then grinned. "I did what I had to do. Growing up with four brothers taught me how to handle bullies. Brains win out over brawn any day of the week."

"Okay," he said, bracing his elbow for another go-around. "Best two out of three."

And he didn't mean arm wrestling. Two could play this game. If she wanted to cheat with a kiss, he would show her how it was done.

Before she could answer, he heard a burst of applause from the doorway. When he whirled around, he saw Nick, Joe and Luke, with his mother and father standing just in front of their sons. All of them were grinning at him as if he'd won first prize at the state fair.

Flo Marchetti walked over to the island and kissed his cheek. "If you can't stand the heat, get out of the kitchen, dear."

Chapter Six

*H*eat? Kitchen? Out?

Sounded good to Fran. In fact, out had been her first choice the moment her sensual haze cleared. Her intention had been to surprise him in order to win. But she'd been the one surprised—at the powerful passionate punch she'd received from the touch of her mouth to his. *Wow* didn't do her feelings justice, but it was the first word that came to mind.

Then she'd realized that Alex's family had seen her kiss him. Correction, not the whole family, just the ones who got a vote. It was the first time since culinary school that she'd been grateful for the tough, character building experience. She'd developed a spine that had kept her rooted to the spot when Alex had introduced her to his parents, Flo and Tom Marchetti.

Since starting at the company five weeks before, she couldn't remember seeing all four of the Marchetti brothers together. Until now. And there should be a law against the phenomenon, because so much masculinity and testosterone in one room could generate a rapturous feminine whimper heard around the world. Even *she* couldn't quite suppress an appreciative sigh. All the brothers had the same dark, wavy hair and eyes. Correction, Luke's eyes were blue. But the olive skin tone was the same. All were tall and muscular and good-looking enough to tempt a convention of card-carrying, man-hating spinsters.

But Alex was by far the best looking.

The fact that Fran could form that thought through her profound embarrassment in front of his family was a testament to her character. Although it was her own fault. She *had* cheated. But damn his male arrogance. Number one, for putting her original recipe on a back burner. Number two, for underestimating her arm wrestling skills, just because she was a woman.

But her self-righteous anger, adrenaline and sensuous daze had evaporated with the sound of applause from his family.

Now she watched anxiously as his parents and brothers sampled the five entrées she'd heated and lined up on the counter. Steam wafted from each as the aromas mingled in the air.

Nobody said anything, and her tension mounted, along with her uncontrollable urge to fill the strained silence. Don't start babbling, she warned herself, just before the words started pouring out of her mouth.

"I've tried to create the average consumer environment. This is the way the food will taste straight from the microwave," she explained. "Although every oven is different and that qualifier needs to be included in heating instructions on the packaging."

They all nodded. Anxiously, she watched them taste, and again her nerves stretched to the breaking point.

Don't open your mouth, came the caution. But again the message drained through the colander of her brain.

"Consumers are health conscious and knowledgeable about reading labels. I used additives that are safe. Canthaxanthin makes food red and is not harmful as opposed to cochineal, which needs more testing to determine risk factors."

She was rambling and couldn't seem to stop. But no one was saying anything. Oh, where was a muzzle, or a sturdy roll of duct tape when she really needed it? Would she be this keyed up if she could control her need to impress Alex? A moot point, until she found the secret ingredient to a recipe for suppressing anything around him.

"Ammonium alginate stabilizes and thickens. And it's extracted from seaweed."

Flo scooped up a forkful of the stuffed shells. After chewing thoughtfully, she said, "Then this one needs more seaweed. It's too watery."

The comment was directed at Alex, and Fran jumped to his defense. "I put too much of the chemical in and it threw the taste off. By the way, don't let the word *chemical* worry you. It tends to put people off, but technically all foods are made up of chemicals." She paused for breath and twisted her fingers together. "They're a normal product of human metabolism. For instance, lactic acid controls pH and is a preservative."

Joe slapped Alex on the back. "Bet that's a chemical near and dear to your heart," he teased.

"A small case of food poisoning might just teach you some respect." Alex smiled at his brother.

The rest of the Marchettis were intent on the food. After her first taste of the shells, Flo went down the line, nodding approvingly at each other entrée. Then she took a bite of the new recipe. She glanced at her son, then met Fran's gaze. "Mmm. Wonderful light flavor. Very tasty."

The rest of the family tested it and raved. After trying each of the entrées, they compared notes and all were in agreement. Pizza, lasagna, spaghetti and meatballs were a go. The last dish was dynamite and they demanded to know what it was.

Fran almost didn't hear the question. Her gaze was glued to Alex, trying to gauge his reaction. Did he share the family's approval? Did he approve of her?

Finally it registered that they were waiting for an answer. "It's angel hair with walnut sauce," Fran explained.

Flo nodded. "I wondered what that flavor was, and the powdered flecks in the sauce. It's marvelous."

"Thank you," Fran said.

"But I give the shells a thumbs-down," she said.

Nick set his fork on the plate in the center of the island. "The dish is substandard," he agreed. "Fran, you've got to improve the texture or it won't go in the launch."

Luke nodded. "No doubt about that."

"How many versions have you done?" Joe asked.

Furtively, she glanced at Alex again to see how he was receiving the evaluation. He looked serious. Angry? Hard to tell. But it was a good bet that she would be cleaning out her desk before the night was over.

"That's number eight," she answered.

Nick frowned. "Overall, it's one of the restaurant's best sellers. But it can't go in the inaugural campaign."

"Not like this," Tom Marchetti agreed. "But after that many attempts without better results, I'm not sure..." He shook his head.

Fran was sure. Women weren't given second chances in this male-dominated industry. In her experience they were expected to do the job twice as well in half the time just to keep working. She'd known from the beginning that the dish wouldn't cut it. She'd also known before the beginning how much Alex wanted his family's approval on this project. And it had gone very well—at least four out of five. But he'd wanted it perfect. She could stand the heat. But she would probably get out of the kitchen. Or rather, be asked to leave. She was the perfect scapegoat for Alex. An inexperienced woman. She would take the rap. After all, the others were family. He had to play nice because he couldn't fire them.

Alex finished up his own taste testing by sampling her new dish. He hadn't tried it before. In spite of waiting for the other shoe to fall, she couldn't help hoping that he liked it. After all, the way to a man's heart… Nope. She wasn't going down that primrose path. Not ever again.

"This *is* good." Alex took another bite. "Really delicious."

"Thank you." Fran untied her apron and slipped it off. "I guess you don't need me any longer. You'll want to talk frankly among yourselves."

It would be less awkward if she left the room while they discussed letting her go. Alex could blame her for everything that was wrong. Although she'd thought he was different. Was it a case of history repeating itself? Had she been temporarily blinded by a good-looking guy who wore wire-rimmed glasses? Another mistake?

Alex blocked her exit. "Not so fast. You need to be here for this."

So, he was going to let her take the blame *and* rub

her nose in it. She had no defense. These people were his flesh and blood. Whose side were they going to take? His, of course. Self-righteous indignation would just be humiliating.

Alex cleared his throat and looked around at the members of his family. "First of all, thank you for coming. Second, I think we're in agreement on the entrées to be included in the launch of Marchetti's Frozen Meals. Pizza, spaghetti and meatballs, lasagna."

He took a breath. "About the shells…"

Here it comes, Fran thought, bracing herself. She felt like a lamb led to slaughter.

"They're out and angel hair with walnut sauce is the replacement."

Fran nearly sustained whiplash as she turned her head to meet his gaze. "What?"

One corner of his mouth turned up. "Your recipe is as good as you said. Better." He glanced back at his family, all of whom were staring at the two of them with indulgent smiles. "Fran said the dish has very few ingredients and is labor light for maximizing profit margin."

"Music to my ears," Luke commented. He was the company's chief financial officer.

"I hear that," Nick agreed.

Joe grinned. "It doesn't hurt that it tastes really good, either."

"True," Alex agreed. "Fran told me the shells wouldn't work."

"So why did you bother with it?" Flo asked him.

"It does seem like a waste of time," his father added.

Program note, Fran thought. Scene two was where the chef goes out on a limb. Solo.

"I'll admit it wasn't my finest hour," he confessed. "As soon as she looked at the recipe she knew. I'm paying the expert for her expertise, and refused to listen. I didn't plan to have the fifth entrée in the tasting."

Fran was stunned. He'd told the truth.

"What made you change your mind?" Nick asked.

"Arm wrestling," Alex said. "She beat me."

Fran moved over on her limb, mentally speaking. And made room for Alex. "I cheated," she explained.

"Bested by a girl," Joe teased. "How dumb is that?"

"Play nice, Joseph Paul," Flo said.

"Uh-oh, when she uses both names, you know you're in trouble," Joe said, winking at Fran.

"If you're not nice," Alex taunted, "I won't solve your problem, as in the food for your wedding. The Marchetti rumor mill has it that you and Liz haven't settled the food portion of your wedding program yet."

"Don't rush into anything," Luke said, jumping on the bandwagon. "The wedding is three whole weeks away."

Joe looked sheepish. "We've been busy. I know," he said, nodding as if he was waiting for the insults to fly. "You'd think someone in the food service industry could get his act together. Yada yada. The fact remains that we have procrastinated."

"Fran is the perfect woman," Alex said. "To do the food, I mean."

Fran glowed, and it wasn't just the lingering effects of his kiss, although his mouth packed a wallop. But his praise filled up a hole in her soul.

"Surely one of the chefs from the restaurants can handle it," she said.

Joe shrugged. "Yeah. But anyone who can make

frozen food taste this good is a culinary genius, and we want you. Besides, if you handle the food, Alex will have a date. Assuming you're not married, engaged or otherwise spoken for.''

"I'm not, but—"

"It's a Wednesday," he continued. "So we're keeping it small. What do you say? Will you do the food for us? Will you take pity on Alex so he won't be alone for an important event like my wedding and Valentine's Day?''

Not only was she not fired, she'd picked up another gig. Would wonders never cease? She smiled. "I'd be happy to. At least the food part," she said, glancing a little shyly at Alex. He was too busy glaring at his brother to notice her. "Why don't I meet with you and Liz together so we can iron out the details? Like making sure she agrees with your choice of caterer?''

Joe grinned. "She will. But I'll call you to set up a time.''

"Wonderful," Flo said. "It's a good thing Joe is charming. It mitigates his less attractive qualities. Like picking on his brother. Although Alex *is* too serious," she added.

"He's pretty charming when he wants to be," Fran blurted.

She didn't miss the gleam in Flo's eyes. The next thing she knew Alex's mother had hustled the family tasters toward the exit.

"Our work here is done," she said. "Alex and Fran have things to do. Let's leave them alone.''

Like a mother hen, Flo easily dispatched her six-foot-plus, husky chicks out the door. After hastily murmured goodbyes, the Marchetti men, plus parents, were gone.

Except one man. Fran looked up at him, at his sensuous mouth, and her knees went weak. "Subtle, aren't they?" she said a little breathlessly.

"About as subtle as a flash flood. Matchmaking is contagious. My mother caught it from Rosie."

"You know your family means well. They just want you to be as happy as they are."

"And they believe there's someone out there for me."

If Fran's hunch was right, they believed she was that someone. But they were wrong. And he wasn't looking. He had found the woman he wanted, one who'd looked forward to marriage, motherhood and being a wife. Fran wasn't even close to that description. Although there were times, like that magical moment when the touch of his lips had made her femininity stand at attention and beg for more, that she wished she could be the kind of woman he would be attracted to.

"Look on the bright side. It would appear that your family is as proud of you as you are of them. You've met your goal."

"Thanks to you." He pushed his glasses up on his nose, then leaned back against the counter. He folded his arms over his chest and rested one loafered foot over the other ankle. "I should have listened to you in the first place. However, arm wrestling is an interesting negotiating technique. We could do a whole management seminar on it."

He meant the kiss. Her stomach fluttered, followed by a sensory memory that gave new definition to the term spontaneous combustion. That touch of his mouth was like throwing kerosene on her simmering attraction. Now it threatened to burn out of control. This was a fine kettle of fish. What was she going to do? She had almost two months left on her contract. She was locked in for at least that long. She had to see him every day at work. Meaning she was in so deep it would take more than an ice cream scoop to dig her out.

She had learned the hard way that if a guy was interested in her, he probably thought she could do something for him, or he wanted her to take the fall for something he had done. She had promised herself that no one would use her again. Now here was Alex. Vice president in the food preparation industry, with his professional reputation at stake, in front of his family, no less. What was she supposed to make of the fact that he hadn't thrown her to the wolves? And he didn't even pretend to be romantically interested in her. If her reaction to that kiss was anything to go by, she *wanted* him to be interested. She was on very thin ice here.

"I thought you were going to fire me."

"For cheating at arm wrestling?"

"That," she agreed. "And for what went wrong with that entrée. I thought you would hang me out to dry."

He frowned. "What have I done to make you believe that?"

"Nothing," she admitted. "But I've got baggage."

"Interesting share. Yet somehow incomplete," he said. "Do you feel like telling me the whole story?"

"No. But I think I owe you an explanation." She twisted her hands together. "In cooking school, I fell for this guy. He was charming and he turned it on full blast. I fell like a cake without baking soda. I didn't know he was using me, copying my work, stealing my notes, et cetera. I thought he cared for me."

"I'm sorry."

"That's not the worst. We had an assignment to make bread. Instead of coming up with his own recipe, he bought a loaf of sourdough and pretended it was original. When one of the instructors caught on, he begged me to take the fall. He was in danger of being thrown out of school and I was at the head of the class. He said I could handle the heat. I did as he asked and was nearly kicked out. My career could have been over before it ever started."

"He must have been grateful."

"Yeah. Right," she said bitterly. "So grateful he dumped me. I found out that he didn't have time to do the work because he was involved with someone else."

"Bastard," Alex said angrily.

"I'll buy that. But I blame myself, too. I was so unbelievably blind. Oh, he said all the right things, paid me compliments. Only later I realized that it was as if an alarm on his watch beeped, telling him it was time to patronize me with flowery words. It just makes me angry that I was so completely gullible."

"Not all guys are insincere creeps." Alex stuck his hands in his pockets.

Maybe. But it hurt too much to try, then be disillusioned. She preferred to take herself out of the game.

"It doesn't matter whether they are or not. I'm not interested in anything serious. Every cloud has a silver lining," she said, trying to smile. "That experience reminded me not to ignore myself in favor of a man. It underscored what I learned growing up—a relationship makes a woman lose herself."

He shook his head. "That's not the lesson. Two people who love each other are stronger together than they are separately."

"Like you and Beth?" she asked.

When would she learn to think before she opened her mouth and let the wrong words out? She waited for the pained expression to cross his face, and was surprised when it didn't.

"Yes, like that," he answered. "The guy was a creep, Fran. It's as simple as that."

"The fact remains that I cared for him. I did things for him that I shouldn't have. I lost myself because of love. And it won't happen again."

"Didn't you tell me that your father knows nothing about this?" he asked.

"Do I have Stupid written on my forehead?" she retorted.

"Maybe he would get off your back about the whole marriage thing if you told him."

She shook her head. "It would just make things worse. First he would track the guy down and defend my honor. Then he would turn over what was left of the jerk to my brothers. After that, he would assume the right to pick out a husband for me, since my judgment leaves something to be desired." She shuddered. "Trust me, it's better if he doesn't find out."

"I guess you know best."

She glanced at her wristwatch. "Wow, look at the time. I've got to clean up and get out of here. I have to shop for my mother. Tomorrow is her birthday and there's a family get-together."

"I'll help you."

"The only way you could help me is by coming along to take the heat off," she said without thinking.

"Actually, I meant help you clean up here. But okay. I'd like to meet your family."

Fran had started gathering up the plates and utensils. She stopped and stared at him. "You're not serious."

"Sure I am. I'm not too proud to help with the dishes."

She shook her head. "No. I meant about meeting my family."

"Yeah, I was serious about that."

"But they're all going to be there. My four brothers, Mom and Dad. That's a lot of Carlinos."

"Why is it so hard for you to believe that I would sincerely like to meet the entire clan?"

She felt his forehead. "No fever. That means you need your head examined."

"Why?"

"It would be like walking into matchmaking central. Voluntarily." She shuddered at the thought as she put the dishes in the sink and went back to the counter for more.

"Hey, turnabout is fair play," he said, picking up the dirty forks and putting them in the sink. He looked down at her. "You've put up with it from the meddling Marchettis. I think it's my turn. Besides, after our triumph with the tasting, I owe you."

She put her hand on her hip and shot him a skeptical look. "They'll try to make us a couple. You will be pumped for information. How long have we known each other? What are your intentions? How far have you gone? Have you kissed me?"

"We both know who kissed who," he said, lifting an eyebrow.

"Okay, I cheated. I'll do penance for it." She was already paying. She could hardly look at him, at his mouth, without wanting to challenge him to a rematch in which she fully intended to cheat by kissing him for all she was worth. She would have to get over it. "But my family doesn't need to know I cheated and how. In fact, it's best if they receive no encouragement. The slightest bit of information would produce a feeding frenzy.''

"What's your point?"

"The Carlinos are not subtle."

"And my family is?"

"Compared to mine? Yes," she said, nodding.

He laughed. "They can't be that bad."

"You'd be surprised. They can be worse. You really don't have to do this."

"What are you afraid of?" he asked.

"Nothing," she said too quickly.

Would she go to hell for the lie? Was lying worse than cheating? It was self-protection. She was trying to prevent emotional suicide. Bad enough that she had to see him every day at work. Somehow she would find a way to withstand his triple threat: laughs, looks and lots of sex appeal. To introduce him to her family was taking a step that scared her. It wasn't business anymore.

"Then what's the problem?" he asked. "If you're looking for a bodyguard, I'm your guy. I'm the perfect man. The meddling Marchettis have trained me for this all my life. Who could understand better than me?"

"I'm just trying to warn you. My father and brothers have frightened off even the most intrepid man who mistakenly thought he could handle escorting me to a Carlino celebration. They can scatter suitors faster than you can say 'Welcome to the family.'"

"I'm not a suitor. I had my shot at romance. I've built up antibodies. I'm immune to whatever the Carlinos can chuck at me."

She put a fork in the automatic dishwasher. "You're sure about this?"

"Absolutely."

It *would* be nice to have some backup tomorrow. And he was right. There was no danger of losing herself, because he'd made it perfectly clear that he wasn't on the make. So what *was* the problem?

"Okay," she said. "You can come." She wagged a finger at him. "But don't say I didn't warn you."

Chapter Seven

After picking Fran up at her apartment, Alex drove
to her parents' house in Woodland Hills, an exclusive
area of the San Fernando Valley. He went slowly up
the street, waiting for her to give him the high sign
when they got to the right house.

Finally she pointed. "This is it."

He couldn't see the place. It was set back from the
road. "Where?"

"Just make a left into the drive and park behind the
last car."

He followed her instructions. But the last car in the
circular drive was a truck, in a line of five trucks that
all sported Carlino Construction on the side. Correction: one was a sports utility vehicle, but still big
enough to curl its bumper in disdain at his small, sporty
two-door. His car looked like an insignificant, incomplete afterthought at the tail end of all the macho
wheels.

After shutting off the engine, he looked over at Fran.

Wearing blue jeans and a pullover sweater in a deep shade of rose, she looked so cute he almost called her Frannie. He remembered Rosie telling him that she hated the nickname, but once again he had to admit his sister was right. It did fit his favorite chef. Although he wouldn't say his sister was right about Fran being the perfect woman. He'd already lost Beth. Only once in a lifetime could the perfect woman find the way to his heart.

Which was why his profound reaction to kissing Fran the day before had shaken him to the core. It had taken all of a second after her lips touched his for his heart rate to zoom off the chart. It had taken him a lot longer to catch his breath. In fact, whenever he was around her, he couldn't swear that it *was* back to normal.

During the sleepless night that followed, he'd told himself she'd just taken him by surprise with her kiss attack. And he almost believed that. In fact, he was choosing to believe it. Because he was tired of all the questions. It was Saturday. They were off work. And he found himself looking forward to spending the rest of the day with her, even if it *was* to run interference with her family.

"Are you ready?" Fran asked him.

"Not if cars are an indicator," he said, pushing his glasses up more securely on his nose. "I'm definitely out of my league."

"It's not too late to back out," she said, grinning.

For the umpteenth time since picking her up, Alex noticed her mouth. He knew now how sweet she tasted, how soft she was. And he wanted to kiss her again. That healthy dose of disloyalty to the love he'd lost was followed by guilt.

He shook his head. "Marchettis are not cowards."

She opened her car door. "Okay. C'mon, hero. Let's do it."

Alex went around to her side. She was holding a plastic container with the birthday cake that she'd made for her mom, and he took it from her. Then she reached into the rear seat, a generous description for his car, he thought wryly, and retrieved the present she'd bought for her mother. With the cake in one hand, he rested his other at the small of her back, and a jolt of electricity zinged him from the innocent touch. It was a good thing he had only one free hand. That was all that prevented him from pulling her into his arms for a repeat kiss.

Fortunately it was just a short distance to the brick-covered front step. The sturdy-looking oak door was inset with leaded, beveled glass etched with flowers. Pretty impressive, he thought.

Fran knocked loudly just before she opened the door to let them in. "Hello," she called out. "Ma? Daddy?"

"In here," a female voice answered.

They walked over the wooden entryway floor. An archway to their left opened to a large kitchen with an oak table and eight ladder-back chairs in the nook. White shutters topped by a blue floral valance covered the windows. Country art and dried flowers decorated the walls. An older woman stood a few feet away by the stove, her wooden spoon poised over a steaming pot. She was about Frans's height, but plump, with gray-streaked brown hair. She must have turned toward the doorway when her daughter had called out because expectation was clearly written on her face.

"Francesca," she said, smiling with pleasure.

"Hi, Ma. Happy birthday." She moved into the woman's arms for a hug.

Her mother met his gaze. "This must be Alex. And he brought a cake."

Fran half turned to include him. "Alex Marchetti, my mother—Aurora Carlino."

"It's nice to meet you," he said, holding out his hand. Then he set the cake on the counter beside the stove. "Fran made the cake, Mrs. Carlino."

"I knew that. Call me Aurora." She put her sturdy hand in his. "The pleasure is mine, Alex. Welcome to our home. I'll get my husband and sons for you to meet."

"Wait, Ma." Fran put her arm around her mother's shoulders. "Why don't we give Alex a breather before we bring on Act Two?" She frowned. "The boys are here. Why are you in the kitchen?"

"Because the boys are here." The woman shrugged, raised her eyebrows and managed to look nonchalant all at the same time. "Why wouldn't I be in the kitchen? I'm cooking dinner for my family."

"But it's your birthday, Ma. Daddy and the boys shouldn't be letting you work today. The least they could have done is order in. You should be pampered."

"I don't mind. It's what—"

"Give me that spoon," Fran said, taking it from her mother.

"About time you got here, Francesca Isabella." A rugged, older-looking man stood in the doorway at the far end of the room. He was taller than Alex, about six foot three, and had a full head of thick, wavy gray hair. "You can take over for your mother. Put to good use what you learned at that hoity-toity cooking school."

"Hi, Daddy," she said. She walked over to him and

kissed his cheek, but Alex didn't miss the way her shoulders tensed, or the tight look around her mouth.

"How are you, cupcake?" he asked, giving her a fond bear hug. "Aren't you going to introduce me to your young man?"

Alex saw her stiffen more. Here we go, he thought. Time to throw a block. He walked forward. "Alex Marchetti, Mr. Carlino. Nice to meet you." He felt his hand squeezed in a viselike grip.

"Leonardo Carlino," Fran's father answered. "How did you meet my Frannie?"

Alex glanced at her and wondered how she could stiffen any more without breaking. He wanted to push her behind him, or better yet, fold her in his arms for safekeeping. But he met her father's gaze and said, "We work together. She's creating recipes for my company."

The older man pointed. "You're the frozen food fella she told us about."

"Will wonders never cease," Fran muttered. "He actually listened."

Alex shot a quick look at her, noticing that her tense shoulders were now nearly around her ears. He winked at her, then smiled at her father. "Yes, sir. I'm the frozen food fella."

"How long have you and Frannie been going out?" Aurora asked.

Alex expected fireworks from his chef, but all he saw was steam. Or maybe that was from the pot she was stirring. But in the time he'd known her, she'd never been so quiet. She always spoke her mind loud and clear. It was one in a long list of things he admired about her. And he missed her biting wit now. But before he could answer the question directed at him, four guys wandered into the room. Alex guessed that these were "the boys." He wasn't sure what he'd expected, but four burly, athletic-looking guys hadn't exactly come to mind.

"Hey, Frannie," the first one said, grabbing her up in his arms. "How are you?"

"I'm fine, Max," she answered, giving him a squeeze.

One by one, each brother bear-hugged her, wooden spoon and all. They looked to be in their late twenties or early thirties, and every last one was at least as tall as their father. If Alex didn't know better, he would swear all of them spent their waking hours working out.

In their Carlino uniform of T-shirt and jeans it was easy to see that each had impressive-looking upper body strength. Every last one had their father's dark brown eyes and thick, wavy black hair. If the entertainment business had been their calling, he hadn't a doubt that Hollywood would embrace them with open arms. Not to mention a good portion of the female population in general.

"Who's this, Sis?" the one who looked to be oldest asked.

"Frannie, introduce your young man to your brothers," her mother ordered.

"He's not my..." She sighed heavily and shook her head. "I'll go in birth order." She pointed with her wooden spoon at a man with a small uneven scar on his chin. "This is my oldest brother, Max. Beside him is Mike, who got all the family charm and people skills," she said, pinching his cheek fondly. "He reminds me of your brother Joe," she said, glancing at Alex. "Next is Sam, the smart one."

"And what are the rest of us? Chopped liver?" Max asked good-naturedly.

"Yes," she said sweetly. "And last but not least is my brother John."

"Hey, I've got people skills," he said.

She grinned at him. "Yes, you do. As long as those people are female." She met Alex's gaze. "Johnny Carlino is the brooding bad boy of the family. Women love him and throw themselves at him on an annoyingly regular basis, in embarrassingly large numbers. But he's not interested and he won't tell me why." She pointed her spoon at Alex. "Although if you have a change of heart about looking, he could give you a refresher course."

"Why would he be looking?" her father asked. "He's got you."

"He doesn't have me—"

Before she could finish her rebuttal or get a really good mad going, Johnny grabbed her around the waist and lifted her easily off her feet. "When I meet a lady as smart and pretty as my little sister, maybe I'll think twice. And if she's as good a cook—"

"Put me down," she said, slapping his hands. "Women have more to offer than preparing meals, you know."

"Yeah," Sam agreed. "You keep reminding us about that."

"For all the good it's done the lot of you. I don't understand how you've all managed to stay unattached," she said, smiling fondly at the group.

"Speaking of attached, you haven't completed the introductions. Who's the guy?" Max asked.

"We're not attached. And this is Alex Marchetti—"

"The frozen food fella?" Mike Carlino asked.

"That's me," Alex agreed.

"Where are your manners, you guys?" Fran asked. "Were you raised by wolves? Isn't it time to do the handshake thing? Or the grunting, bonding and back slapping that goes along with it?"

Sam tugged a lock of her hair. "You have to get over this need you have to stereotype, Sis."

She shrugged. "What can I say? I'm a product of my environment."

Alex wondered if he was the only one who got the hidden zinger. Her environment had been filled with love. No doubt about that. And not so subtle pressure, if the last few minutes were anything to judge by. Her parents wanted him and Fran to be a couple. But he'd been warned about that.

One by one "the boys" stuck out their hands for Alex to shake. "Nice to meet you," he said, suppressing the urge to flex his fingers after the workout his hand had gotten.

Leo Carlino cleared his throat. "We're missing the football game. It's on in the other room. Come join us, Alex."

Alex looked at Fran and almost winced at the anxiety, abandonment and anger that darkened her eyes. If he had to guess, he would bet she was fried about being relegated to the kitchen, as if by virtue of her gender that's where she belonged. He also knew she wouldn't walk away and leave her mother here to cook.

"Is there anything I can do to help?" he asked Aurora.

Before she could speak, Leo answered. "Leave this to the women."

"Thank you, Alex," Aurora said. "My daughter and I can take care of things. You would just be in the way.

Join the men. Everything will be ready in about a half hour.''

He looked at Fran, studying her for a reaction.

She nodded. "It's okay, Alex."

But she didn't look okay and he had to fight the urge to fix that.

After dinner, everyone withdrew to the family room for cake. On the tour of the house, Max had explained to Alex that this had once been a tandem, three-car garage. They had converted it into an L-shaped room large enough for a fireplace with raised, used-brick hearth, and a billiards table on the other side, sort of around the corner. There was a grouping of leather sofas and blue-and-green plaid wing chairs, with a coffee table in the center. In the corner was a big screen TV. They had almost completely remodeled the house, which was large and elegant, yet homey and comfortable. He could see why Carlino construction was so successful.

While they waited to do the birthday cake, everyone sat around chatting.

"Did you get approval on those plans you drew up for that office building in Santa Monica?" Leo asked. "Max is an architect," he confided to Alex.

His oldest son nodded. "The CEO only had two or three changes. I thought it was going to take a couple more passes before we got the go-ahead."

"Good." Leo smiled approvingly.

"I had a really good week, too," Fran said. She sat on the end of the sofa across from him, sticking candles in the cake. "The Marchettis approved my variation of their restaurant recipes for the launch of their frozen food campaign."

"Ahead of schedule, too," Alex interjected.

"That's good," Leo said absently. "Mike, what about an estimate for that strip mall in Thousand Oaks? Did you give them a bid?"

Alex saw the disappointment on Fran's face, and her shoulders drooped as her father brushed her off. She got up and left when he directed his attention to his second-born son.

"Sure did, Dad. But no decision yet. They have to take ours to the board along with two others. If I had to guess, I'd say we've got a good shot at it."

"Nice job, son."

Fran reentered the room with dessert plates and forks. "Dad, did I tell you how much everyone liked the original recipe I created? The Marchettis unanimously agreed to include it in the first entrées that go on the market. When I add that to my résumé, it will do a lot for my career—"

"Career? Cooking?" Leo smiled indulgently.

"I'm making a living," she reminded him.

He shrugged, then glanced at Alex as he raised one eyebrow. "A husband and family. Now that's living." Then he turned his attention to his third born. "Sam, can you put together the crew? If we get that Santa Monica project, we're going to need the best to bring that building in on time and within budget."

His son nodded. "If we get the go-ahead, I'll find the manpower we need."

"I don't know how you manage it, son, but you always seem to get the job done."

Alex thought Fran looked shell-shocked or steam-rollered as she sat on the end of the sofa and lit the birthday candles on the cake. When she completed the task, everyone sang "Happy Birthday" to Aurora.

"My job is going really well," Fran said when there was quiet again. She'd pulled herself together for another shot at her share of the attention. "Alex and I—"

"Speaking of Alex," her father said, looking at him. "What do you think of my Frannie? She's a good cook, don't you agree?"

"Dad, don't put him on the spot," she pleaded.

"If I didn't, she wouldn't be working for me." Alex smiled at her as he took the cake she handed him. "Your daughter is very good at what she does. She's got a knack for adapting recipes, not to mention creating her own. She has the potential for a long and successful career in the food service industry," he added, meeting her father's gaze.

Alex held his temper—barely. He was angry that no one stood up for her. Everyone ignored her achievements. No wonder she was antirelationship and marriage. No wonder she shied away from giving her heart to a man. She feared she would lose herself in the process. He was here to run interference and, by God, that's what he would do.

"Thanks to Fran, we have a very good chance of getting a hefty share of the four-*billion*-dollar-a-year frozen food market," he said. He glanced around at the members of her family and watched as all their eyebrows raised like a stadium of fans doing the wave.

"Did you say billion?" Leo asked.

"You heard right. I aim to grab a hefty share of that market. But I couldn't do it without Fran. You should be very proud of her."

"She sure knows her way around a kitchen," Leo agreed. "She'll make someone a good wife. When she walks down the aisle to her husband someday, it will make me very proud."

Alex almost lost it. He wanted to shake the man until his teeth rattled. He looked at Fran and noticed the high color in her cheeks. She seemed to shrink into herself, and he knew she'd given up. The little-girl-lost look tugged at his heart.

"Frannie, why don't you finish cutting your mother's cake?" Leo said. "Everyone has to have at least a bite or it's bad luck."

Without a word, she did as he asked, and passed around the plates. She took one bite and set her plate on the coffee table.

Alex tasted the black forest cake and felt like he'd died and gone to heaven. "Fran, this is really good," he said. "We may have you create a line of frozen desserts, too."

"Thanks, Alex," she answered, without her characteristic spirit.

He waited for everyone to compliment her. They all nodded agreement, but no one said anything. Anger coursed through him.

Alex finished his cake and put his plate on the table. "Do you have any idea how talented Fran is? Not just any chef—man or woman—could do what she did—"

"Do you know how to shoot pool?" Fran interrupted him.

"Yes." He knew she was distracting him, and suspected she was heading him off from a family confrontation. He took a deep breath, releasing some of his annoyance. "Does that table over there really work or is it just a decoration?"

"It's fully functioning."

"Watch out, Alex," Max interjected. "Frannie goes for the jugular."

"He's not kidding," Sam added. "She's good. Watch out or she'll beat the pants off you."

Alex laughed, then met Fran's gaze. "Are you challenging me to a game?"

"I am," she answered, standing.

"Then I should warn you. I was the pool champion of my fraternity house in college." He put his empty plate on the coffee table and stood up, following her.

"If you're trying to intimidate me, I should tell you it's a waste of time," Fran said, handing him a cue stick. "I have nerves of steel."

"So I noticed," he said, nodding in the direction of the Carlino clan conversing on the other side of the room.

She shook her head slightly and said, "Do you want to break or should I?"

"Are you going to cheat?" Alex asked with a small smile.

If it involved kissing, he hoped she would cheat big time. The mere thought made his pulse do a jig, and he grew hot all over.

"I don't have to cheat," she answered, eyes sparkling. "Winning isn't based on strength, but skill. And I have enough to beat you fair and square."

"Okay. How would you like to put your money where your mouth is?" he asked.

Why had he said that? He was his own worst enemy when it came to Fran's irresistible lips.

"You're on. How much?"

"A buck."

"Wow, you're really sure of yourself, aren't you?" she teased.

"I'm walking a fine line here," he explained. "I

don't want to take too much from a lady on a budget. But the bet has to be enough to preserve your pride."

She laughed. "Just don't you worry your pretty little head about my pride. It's yours that will be needing a trip to the trauma center in a few minutes."

"Okay. Ladies first," he said. "You break."

She grabbed the triangular shaped rack and put the striped and solid-colored balls inside, pushing it back and forth several times to keep them in formation. Then she removed it.

"You're sure you want me to go first?" she asked archly. "It does give me the advantage. And a dollar is a mighty powerful motivator."

"I'm absolutely positive."

She bent over the table, giving him a spectacular view of her rear end. And what a work of art it was. Encased in denim, she had curves that made his palms itch to touch her. He couldn't classify her body language as a deliberate cheat, but she'd distracted him just the same. And he felt his hands shaking. It was time to level the playing field.

At the same moment she drew her elbow back to take the shot, he said, "Don't rush, Fran. Take your time."

She jerked her arm, but didn't touch the ball. Then she straightened and smiled sweetly. But there was a challenging expression in her eyes that thrilled him. "You know, Alex, retaliation is a petty, ugly thing. Beneath you, I'd say."

He would go to his grave without explaining that his motive wasn't revenge so much as making the most of this opportunity to gaze a little longer at her shapely fanny. With her four brothers and father just a cue ball's throw away, that confession would never pass his lips.

"You're right. I apologize. Go ahead. I'll be good." He paused. "Frannie."

She straightened again and glared. "Okay. You want to play dirty, I can arrange that."

If "playing dirty" meant kissing, she could count him in. Alex released a long breath. Ever since sampling her lips, all he could think about was Fran for a full course of necking. And the feeling was getting stronger. But his timing couldn't be worse, what with her bodyguard brothers close by. He could probably handle them one at a time. He wasn't chief financial officer for the company, but even he knew that four-to-one odds were not in his favor. Actually, it was five to one if you included Leo, who was still in good shape for an older guy.

"Define 'playing dirty,'" Alex said.

She slanted him a narrow-eyed gaze. "It's the glasses that confused me. They make you look so bright. I'm saying that if you want to keep up the running commentary to throw me off—"

"Throw you off?" he asked, raising an eyebrow.

"I won't stoop to calling it cheating," she said loftily. "But if you want to keep up the chatter, that's fine and dandy. Be prepared for a sneak attack in return. And you know I'm just the woman who can do it."

Yes, indeed. The perfect woman. He dismissed that thought even as his blood hummed through his veins at the very idea. His heart kicked up a sensuous rhythm, and sweat popped out on his forehead. What was wrong with him? He didn't just mean the fact that he wanted to neck with her right here under the watchful eye of testosterone times five.

He was amazed that he'd thought of it at all. One little kiss had changed everything. Not only had it made him hot all over, but he'd begun to question his loyalty to the memory of his lost love. Did Beth even deserve his loyalty any longer?

"Yes, you're just the woman—"

Alex stopped when he heard Fran mumble something under her breath. He saw her frown, then followed her gaze. Aurora was piling up dirty dishes.

Fran leaned her cue against the table and moved toward her family in the other part of the room. "Hold that thought," she said to him.

"With pleasure," he answered softly.

"Ma, what are you doing?" She took dessert plates from her mother, who was gathering them together.

"I'm just cleaning up. Go back to your game. Entertain Alex," she said.

"It's your birthday," Fran reminded her. "This is your day and you don't need to do for everyone else." She stacked the dirty plates and forks on the coffee table. "Sit down and relax. I'll take care of these and the rest of the kitchen."

Her mother smiled at her. "All right. But while I'm up, does anyone want anything?" she asked the semicomatose men.

"I'd like a glass of milk," Max said.

Fran huffed out an impatient breath. Then she looked at her mother. "I'll get it. Sit down, Ma."

"You're sure, sweetheart?"

"Absolutely."

Fran disappeared with the plates and returned a few moments later with a tall glass of milk. "Here you go, Maximilian."

"Thanks, Sis," he said, absently watching TV. He

glanced at her and said, "Geez, you milked the whole cow. I only wanted half a glass."

Even from across the room, Alex recognized the mutinous expression in Fran's eyes. He held his cue stick and watched with anticipation, waiting to see what was coming. She didn't disappoint.

"Half a glass?" she said with deadly calm.

In the blink of an eye she tipped the glass, dumping the liquid in her brother's lap. As he let out a yelp, she righted it for a moment to assess the remaining contents, then poured a bit more on him. "There, that's one-half," she said, handing him the glass.

"What the hell did you do that for?" he hollered, jumping to his feet.

"Francesca Carlino, what in the world has gotten into you?" her father asked, his voice raised.

"Not fractions. They always were a challenge for me," she said to her father. "In spite of that, I'm just as important as the boys. I do have hopes, dreams and accomplishments—just like them."

Then she turned on her heel and walked out of the house.

Chapter Eight

Fran turned her key in her apartment door and opened it. The two of them had left her parents right after she'd baptized her brother with the milk. She'd apologized to her mother when she'd said goodbye at the door. But she and Alex had hardly spoken on the way home. She hadn't known what to say. Somehow she felt she needed to give him an explanation for her behavior, however.

No matter her attraction, he was her boss. And it was the same old thing. If a male chef acted badly, it was genius. If a female showed temper, she was just a witch having PMS.

She glanced at Alex over her shoulder. "Would you like to come in for a nightcap?"

"Are you going to pour it on me?"

"Only if you make me cook and clean, fetch and carry, and be subservient," she answered shortly.

She knew he was teasing. Bless him, he had done his best to stand up for her in front of the formidable

Carlino clan. He'd gone above and beyond the call of duty and still it hadn't been enough to keep her from snapping.

Why?

She'd been dealing with her family all her life. She was used to them. She'd put up with their matchmaking since she'd passed into what they considered the spinster zone. She couldn't help thinking what a small window of time it was from chaperoning her every waking moment to practically taking out billboards on the San Diego Freeway proclaiming that she was available. And she'd taken it in stride, she thought proudly. But she'd lost her cool tonight, and she knew it had something to do with Alex. Did she actually want the same guy the Carlino clan wanted her to have? Was she, even subconsciously, on their side?

Little did they know that he wasn't interested.

"I'm sorry," she said. "I didn't mean to take out my frustration on you. If I promise not to dump anything on you, would you like to come in?"

Not only because she enjoyed his company, she didn't want to be alone to think about the fact that she was going to hell for what she'd done. And she didn't want to psychoanalyze why she'd done it. She relaxed when he slanted her an easy grin.

"Okay," he agreed. "And you can dump on me if you want. As long as it's words."

It was nice the way he knew that she needed to vent. She wasn't used to anyone, any *guy*, paying that much attention to her.

He followed her into her apartment. "What can I get you?" she asked.

"Something that doesn't stain." He held up his hands at her indignant huff and dramatic eye rolling.

"I'm kidding. How about coffee? I haven't had enough stimulation today."

"Yeah, me neither. My adrenaline certainly hasn't pumped in a while," she joked.

"Just give me a few seconds head start if you decide to pump it in my direction."

"Deal," she said, laughing. "I'll make a pot—coffee, not adrenaline," she clarified.

She pulled the automatic coffeemaker out of the cupboard, then put water in it and measured out fresh grounds. Finally, she plugged it in and flipped the On switch.

She heard the coffeemaker start to sizzle and drip, and realized how glad she was to be home. It was the last week of January and the weather had turned cold. But her cozy apartment wasn't the only thing she was glad about. Being with Alex factored in as well. Not only had he braved spending time with a psychotic woman, but he'd made her laugh, teasing her out of an angry, self-pitying mood.

She finally looked at him, and something about the way he looked back, the spark of intensity mixed with a healthy dose of hunger, made her stomach flutter, her heart race and her thoughts turn to kissing. From there it was a stone's throw to that odd sensation of her toes curling.

He'd sat down on one of her bar stools to watch her in the kitchen. If possible, he was cuter than ever in his worn jeans and preppy pullover sweater, his white shirt collar sticking up from the crew neck. She couldn't see his feet from where she stood, but she remembered that he was wearing loafers. She always remembered the smallest details about Alex.

He hadn't said anything while she'd made the coffee.

It was as if he was giving her space. To cool off? To form her thoughts? Would he have kept quiet if he'd known she wanted him to kiss her again? No matter. Either way, she appreciated his sensitivity.

She could add that to Alex's adjectives, his list of *S* words: *suave, smiling, sad, sexy, sensitive.* And suddenly she had to know something. It had been on her mind since her first day of work at the company. After their kiss yesterday, the answer had taken on monumental importance. Even after tonight's temporary insanity, she still wanted to know. Because she figured her heart was in no danger. He wasn't in the market for love. And what man in his right mind would want a psychotic shrew?

Here goes, she thought.

"What did you do to make it impossible for your secretary to forget me?"

She leaned on the counter, just in front of where he sat at the bar. Looking him straight in the eye, she resisted the urge to sigh adoringly. She just wasn't the adoring type, although Alex was the first man to make her think about changing.

He gave her a blank look. "What?"

"My first day at Marchetti's. I was surprised when your secretary, Joyce, knew me. She remembered my name and said that you'd made it impossible to forget me. What did she mean? What did you do? Why did she say that?"

"Because she's a troublemaker," he said, squirming as he pushed his glasses up on his nose.

Fran shook her head. "I don't believe that for a second, or you wouldn't keep her around."

"Okay."

She waited for him to say more, and wondered why

she didn't let him off the hook. Why did she need the validation? Because she didn't get it from her family? Probably. Because her self-esteem needed shoring up? No doubt. And Alex was just what the doctor ordered, because he wasn't looking for love any more than she was. And after tonight's Carlino catastrophe, she didn't care how pitiful or obvious, she needed a self-confidence booster. She was blatantly fishing for compliments.

"So what did you do?" she prompted, when he wasn't forthcoming.

"I had the Carlino countdown on my calendar," he said.

"You mean you kept track of the days until I started?" At his nod, she continued to fish. "And she looks at your calendar every day?"

"That's what subservient secretaries do," he confirmed. "Besides making coffee," he added, with a twinkle in his eyes.

Fran decided to ignore his barb. "And that's all? You never said or did anything else that would keep me at the forefront of her memory?"

"I might have mentioned your name once or twice, in the two weeks before you started work. Why?" he asked.

She shrugged. "Just curious. I'd been wondering about it and—"

"You're a gifted chef, Fran. I don't have to be psychic to predict a long and stellar *career* for you."

She met his gaze. "What did I do to deserve such a glowing commendation?"

"You spent the day with your family."

She felt the corners of her mouth turn up. Apparently

she was as subtle as her father. Alex had read her easily. Again.

"I'd like to thank you," she said.

"It's nothing more than the truth. You're very good at what you do. And in spite of what your family thinks, it is a career. One that's just as important as what your brothers do."

"Actually, I wasn't talking about the glowing commendation, although I very much appreciate the sentiment. I mean I really *need* to thank you."

"For what?" he asked, puzzled.

"Where do I start?" she said with a sigh. "For coming with me to take the edge off being with my family. For enduring the matchmaking—with good humor, I might add. For trying to defend me."

Especially that. For the rest of her life she would always remember how he'd gone into battle for her. At his own family castle, he might be third son dealing with second-son syndrome, but he was chock-full of chivalry, with a generous dollop of cute.

"Coffee's done," he said, pointing to the electric appliance behind her.

She turned and realized it was, but she'd been too busy worshiping at Alex's feet to notice. Someday soon she would have to do something about the whole adoration thing where he was concerned. She took two mugs from the cupboard, then poured the steaming dark liquid into each. "Do you take it black, or with cream and sugar?" she asked.

"Both," he said. "Although black fits my mood better."

She handed him a cup, retrieved the appropriate condiments for his preference, then curled her hands around her own mug. She watched him spoon sugar and pour cream into his coffee until it was light brown. "You? In a black mood?"

He was the most even-tempered man she'd ever met. It was one of the things she liked best about him.

"It really fried me that they dismissed you out of hand."

"I told you. An engagement ring on my finger is the only thing that will get my father's attention."

"No wonder you're resistive to a serious relationship."

"So you understand now?"

"Oh, yeah," he said. "The thinking is so Middle Ages."

"Unlike second-son syndrome," she teased.

"I thought we agreed that was a by-product of doing the family proud."

"We did. I just couldn't resist. And in spite of the way it looks, they do love me," she said. "Even if I'm not married."

"I never said they didn't. They made their feelings clear. But your accomplishments *are* just as important as your brothers'. No wonder Max is wearing his milk."

Alex understood, she thought. In spite of herself, she released an audible, adoring sigh. "My father will never see cooking as a career choice unless I do it in my husband's kitchen," she said.

"I have a kitchen." He looked surprised, as if he hadn't meant to say that.

"Yes, you do. At work, and probably one at home, too." She blew on her coffee as her heart pounded almost painfully against the wall of her chest. What was he saying? "Is there any reason in particular why you pointed that out to me?"

Frowning, he shook his head. "No. Just my convoluted way of saying that stereotypical typecasting is absurd."

So it wasn't his nebulous way of saying that she could be the special woman in either or both of his kitchens. The stab of disappointment took her completely by surprise, because for so long she had run from wanting a man in her life.

He met her gaze. "What I'm trying to say is that I care about you. I care what happens to you."

"You mean after my commitment with your company is over," she clarified.

"Yes," he agreed. "But I like you, Fran. I want to be your friend."

"What about Beth?" Why had she asked that?

"She'll always be a part of me. I'll never forget her. But I have to move forward."

"So you've changed your mind about looking for love?"

Darn. Fran couldn't seem to stop putting her foot in her mouth. But because her own feelings had shifted, she needed to know where he was coming from.

"No. I already had my chance at that. But it just hit me that I have to move forward with my life without feeling disloyal to her memory every time I enjoy myself."

"And this revelation happened at my folks' house today?" She shrugged. "Funny. I thought I was the one taking the hits. I didn't see the lightning bolt zap you." His grin, so sudden, so appealing, made her want to grip the counter she leaned on, to keep from dissolving into a puddle at his feet.

He tipped his head in a sheepish gesture. "It's hard to explain, but I guess you could say it came over me about the same time you dumped your message on Max,'' he said wryly.

Then, in a roundabout way, she'd helped him, too. ''So is there something you'd like to say?''

He looked puzzled. ''According to my sister there are only two things a woman wants to hear from a man. 'I was wrong' and 'it will never happen again.'''

''No. You need to thank me for exposing you to the Carlinos, who made you appreciate life again.''

''Yeah.'' He nodded. ''Something like that.''

''Then I guess I don't need to explain or apologize for my behavior?''

''I liked your behavior.'' He slanted her a look filled with such longing and desire, it was a good thing the bar separated them. She would have been in his arms, with her mouth on his, before you could say *bon appetit.* She felt the thin barrier of her defenses weakening.

She glanced at her watch. ''Wow. Where has the time gone?''

''I guess that's my two minute warning.''

''It's getting late,'' she agreed.

She walked him to the door and opened it. Part of her wanted to beg him to stay. Part of her was glad he was leaving before her mouth got her into more trouble she would regret.

''I won't say I'm sorry you saw the real me in action tonight, Alex. But I have to thank you for everything you did.''

She stood on tiptoe to kiss his cheek. At the last minute, Alex turned his head and captured her mouth with his. Surprise didn't quite do justice to what Fran felt. A repeat of this performance hadn't been far from her mind, but she'd never expected him to take the lead. Then rational thought receded as the soft, warm touch of his lips did very delicious things to her insides.

Tingles started in her chest and rippled outward, racing down her arms and over her thighs. Her knees threatened to buckle until his strong arm settled comfortably around her waist, gently urging her against his solid length. Almost of their own will, her hands slid up his chest and curved around his neck. Her heart pumped faster, but her breath seemed to collect and stall in her lungs.

Fran pressed closer to him, her breasts flattening against the wall of his chest. She thrilled to the sensation of his arms tightening around her and to the sound of his own unsteady breathing. And all the while his mouth, tender and tantalizing, explored hers.

He upped the stakes when his tongue probed at the seam of her lips. She opened, permitting him access. He caressed the interior, softly, gently, completely. Her blood pounded through her veins and her heart thumped against her chest. Heat radiated through her. When she touched her tongue to his, he sucked in an unsteady breath and pulled her even more firmly to him.

Then he turned his attention to her jaw and nibbled tender kisses down her neck, stopping at a spot just below her ear. Her breasts seemed to swell and grow heavy, and her tingles grew tingles. The air in her lungs released with a frustrated sigh.

He kissed her like a man who knew what he was doing and it was a heady experience. He kissed her deftly and thoroughly, and made her want more. Either he wasn't out of practice as he'd said, or knowing how to please a woman was instinctive for him.

"Fran," he whispered raggedly against her mouth.

He pulled back slightly before resting his forehead against hers. "What was it you said?" he asked, his chest rising and falling rapidly.

It took her several moments to remember. "I believe I thanked you for everything you did."

"You're welcome." He drew in a deep breath.

"But I was premature," she said, trying to steady herself, slow down her pulse. "Now I need to thank you for *that*. I thought you said you didn't date."

"I don't," he said, looking down at her.

"Well, your kisser sure isn't out of practice."

He grinned. "That's the nicest thing you could have said to me."

"Good, because now I want you to leave. And I mean that in the nicest possible way."

He frowned. "Should I say I'm sorry?"

"You're the boss. You tell me."

Somehow she had to get back her professional detachment. Ha! And for her next magical trick maybe she could pull it out of a hat, because she hadn't been emotionally detached since meeting Alex.

He loosened his hold and took a half step back. Then he reached out and tucked a strand of hair behind her ear. His hand was shaking. "I'd be lying if I said I was sorry. See you at work Monday," he said as he opened the door.

"Not if I see you first," she whispered, closing it after him.

By the end of the next week, Alex had decided that while his kisser might not be out of practice, his intuition about women definitely was. It had taken him four workdays to realize that Fran had managed to stay out of his way for all that time, except for brief moments.

He got it when his secretary informed him that Fran had canceled out on their Friday afternoon meeting. She'd gone home early with a headache. And before he could comment, Joyce had confirmed that Fran looked tired and overworked, and a boss in touch with his feminine side would do something nice. Fran's excuse might be legitimate, but it highlighted the fact that he hadn't seen much of her lately and he'd missed her.

He stood outside her door now and wondered what the heck he was doing back at the scene of the crime. He'd kissed her, and he'd liked it. She'd liked it, if his instincts weren't completely rusted out. And there wasn't a doubt in his mind that kissing her had sent her running for cover.

What had possessed him to do it?

Something had shifted for him that day with her family. He'd never felt anything like that need to protect her, not even with Beth. Which was odd since, on the surface at least, Fran was spirited and spunky. Nothing like the woman he'd lost. But somehow, he sensed Fran's vulnerability and how easily she could be hurt. And he didn't want anyone to hurt her. It was damned confusing. Especially why he'd kissed her in the first place.

He considered himself a man of above average intelligence. And he had a fair share of common sense. But when he had been in Fran's apartment, saying good-night, and she'd looked at him with that sexy look she had, the one so hot it could melt butter... He shook his head.

"That's why it's not a good idea to mix business and pleasure," he said to himself.

If he had any sense at all, he would turn around and walk away. Then he made a fist and knocked on her door. Apparently he had no sense. Inside, he heard a slight scraping sound and smiled. She was dragging her step stool to the peephole to check out who was there. Would she open the door when she saw it was him?

Several moments passed, and he thought she was going to ignore him. Then he heard the chain slide from the lock, and the door opened.

She stood there in black sweatpants and a white fleece shirt. Her brown hair was secured on top of her head with a clip. Her creamy skin was completely free of makeup. Dark circles stained the curve beneath her chocolate-colored eyes. And guilt assailed him. Not the kind he used to feel on Beth's account. Thanks to Fran, he wasn't rooted in the past any longer. He knew love wasn't in the crystal ball, but life could still be fun and fulfilling. Like working with Fran, for instance. Although he was afraid he'd been working her too hard in order to get his campaign off the ground. And that was the source of his guilt.

"Hi," he said.

"What are you doing here?" she asked.

"I was worried about you. You called in sick for our meeting today."

"I have a headache."

"So I heard."

"Are you here to check up on me?" she asked.

"I'm here to help." He held out a brown paper bag. "I've brought you the latest headache remedy. It's like an ice pack. You put it on your forehead and it's supposed to soothe."

She took the sack. "Thanks."

She frowned, then winced and touched her fingers to her temple. He kicked himself for letting her put in all the long hours. And he suspected that kissing her had pushed the needle of her stress meter into the red.

"Are you so solicitous of all your employees?" she asked.

"Honestly?" At her nod, he said, "Just the ones who are overworked." And underkissed, he thought.

She looked over her shoulder as if there was someone behind her. "There's no one here who fits that description."

"Would you mind if I come in?" he asked. At her doubtful look, he added, "I won't stay long."

She hesitated only a moment before opening the door wide enough to admit him. "Sorry. Please come in."

"Thanks." He caught the floral scent of her perfume as he passed her.

The fragrance, like a meadow of flowers, would forever bring her to his mind. If he was in a pitch-black room, the scent would lead him straight to her. And finding her mouth would be as easy as falling off a log.

Desire sprang to life and curled inside him. He wanted to hold her again, feel her breasts pressed against his chest, kiss her sensuous mouth and feel her passionate response. Wow, Fran had brought him back to life—all of him, he thought ruefully. But it was only lust, pure and simple. It couldn't be anything else. Curbing it wouldn't be easy, but he would if it killed him. Because in spite of her claim to the contrary, Fran was a forever-after kind of woman. And his chance at love was used up.

But that wasn't why he'd stopped by, he reminded himself. He was being a Good Samaritan.

"I disagree. You fit the classic description of an

overworked employee.'' He took her arm and led her to the sofa.

''And what's that?''

''Cranky, short-tempered and ducking the boss.''

''I'm not,'' she protested. ''I wasn't. I didn't.'' But she couldn't quite look him in the eye.

On the couch, there was a pillow where she'd obviously been resting. ''Lie down,'' he said.

''But—''

''I'm the boss,'' he said firmly. He gently pushed her down, then lifted her legs and swung them around to make her recline. He took the bag from her, opened the package and placed the cool patch on her forehead. ''Now. How does that feel?''

''Mmm,'' she said, closing her eyes. ''Just what the doctor ordered.''

''I'm glad you feel that way, because I've got one more prescription.''

''What?'' she asked. Her eyes snapped open and there was a definite glint of suspicion in them.

''A long weekend in the mountains.''

She started to shake her head, and winced. ''Just pick up and take off? But I can't. I don't have anyplace to stay.''

''My family has a cabin in Big Bear. It was a get-away love nest for my folks when we were kids. Rosie and Steve fell in love there. So did Nick and Abby, if family scuttlebutt can be trusted.''

She smiled. ''I guess you don't go there.''

''No.'' He put keys and written directions on the table. ''And I'm not now. You can have the place all to yourself. Long walks in the fresh air and lots of R and R is what you need. You've been putting in a lot of hours at work and preparing for my brother's wedding on top of that. So off you go for a rest.''

She sat up and her headache patch plopped onto her chest. ''It does sound enticing.''

Not as enticing as holding her in his arms and kissing her until she released her sweet, sexy little sigh that drove him wild. Sweat popped out on his forehead as he stuck his hands in his pockets and backed toward the door.

''No argument,'' he said.

''Okay.''

''Go. Fly. Be free. And don't come back until you're not cranky, short-tempered or ducking the boss anymore.''

The last part was the most important to him.

Chapter Nine

F ran unlocked and opened the cabin door and looked around. A circular brick fireplace sat in the center of the large room. A hunter-green-and-maroon plaid sofa and love seat formed a conversation area on one side, with oak occasional tables arranged around it. Through a doorway to her right, she found the downstairs master bedroom and bath, complete with gold fixtures.

"What a terrific place," she whispered, setting her suitcase down in the room.

She walked back through the main living area to see what the getaway-place kitchen of a restaurant family looked like. Halfway there, she noticed that the carpet felt squishy, and she got that please-God-no feeling in the pit of her stomach. Hurrying the rest of the way, she entered the room and had a general impression of ceramic tile countertops and a center work island before she noticed water pouring out from underneath the sink. It was half an inch deep and spreading steadily.

"Holy smoke. It's a full-fledged flood," she said.

"What do I do now? Duh. That's a no brainer. Stop the water, genius. That's easier said than done. There's never a man around when you need one."

She turned off the water under the sink. Then used a lot of precious time finding a wrench and the main shut-off valve outside. Now what? A quick survey of the downstairs revealed that the living room carpet was saturated. Her first instinct was to call Alex. Her second was no way.

When he'd offered her the cabin, she'd figured he wanted to put some distance between them as much as she did. She couldn't speak for him, but for her it was because of that kiss—and the way it had made her feel. She'd managed to avoid him at work for the last week, mostly because he'd been out of the office a lot. Her headache had forced her to cancel out on the meeting, but then he'd shown up at her apartment with the latest wonder cure. How sweet was that?

Now she was avoiding him in the mountains. Head for the hills had never been more literal. But she felt sure someone in the Marchetti family would want to know their cabin was full of water. It was Saturday so she knew she wouldn't find anyone at the office. Alex's home number was in her organizer, but she'd already established that he wouldn't want to hear from her. Could she get in touch with anyone else? Rosie. She found her friend's business card in her purse, and luckily, her home number was on it, too.

Her footsteps squishing on the watery carpet, Fran located the phone in the living room. The water had risen high enough to wet the fabric on the furniture. And it was oozing farther into the room, causing more damage. At least nothing was floating.

After she tapped in the numbers, the phone rang twice before her friend picked up. "Rosie, it's Fran—"

"Hey, stranger. I heard the tasting was fantastic. My parents raved about you. The whole arm-wrestling thing and the kiss, a stroke of genius—"

"Rosie, listen, there's a problem."

"What?" she asked.

"I'm at your family's cabin in the mountains and I just got here—"

"Great. Tell Alex hi for me. Besides the fact that you're with my brother, what's the problem?"

"Alex isn't here. But water is. Lots and lots." She took a deep breath. "A pipe broke under the kitchen sink and the water is deep enough to do the backstroke. The living room carpet is soaked. I've shut off the water to the house, but I don't know who to call. I can't authorize cleanup and repairs. Not to mention notifying the insurance company. Help—"

"Sit tight. I'll send reinforcements."

"Rosie, don't bother Alex—"

There was a click on the other end of the line, and Fran had a feeling that her friend either hadn't heard or would ignore the last part. But maybe she wouldn't be able to locate him on his day off. There were lots of other family members. Fran had a one-in-seven chance of getting someone besides the man who could make enough at a carnival kissing booth to be comfortable for the rest of his life. There was every reason to believe luck would be on her side.

Two and a half hours later she saw Alex's car stop in front of the cabin, and she made a mental note not to go to Las Vegas anytime soon. Although she tried very hard to shush it, there was a part of her doing a cheer at the sight of him. And not just because of the flood.

He looked good.

She was standing outside on the deck, and watched as he climbed the two flights of wooden stairs to the front door. Fortunately, she'd brought a heavy jacket. She'd known it would be cold, but hadn't expected to be stuck outside while the insurance company water-loss unit worked their magic. She had to admit it was worth all the anxiety to behold the sight of Alex in worn jeans and a blue-and-gray plaid flannel shirt with sleeves rolled up. Beneath it he wore a black Henley undershirt, and she couldn't help thinking he could pass for a lumberjack. Her gaze was drawn to his broad shoulders and wide chest. He had the strength for the job, she thought.

He could fit right in anywhere—backwoods, board-room...bedroom. Don't go there, she warned herself.

"Hi," she said, when he reached her.

"Hi, yourself," he shouted over the sound of the pump motor. He stepped over the cords and lines strewn about the wooden deck.

"The insurance company got a crew here about an hour ago."

He nodded. "It's a national company with a good reputation. They told me on the phone that a special unit would be dispatched right away to minimize damage."

"They're taking care of everything pretty efficiently. As soon as they arrived, I called Rosie to let her know that it wasn't necessary to bother sending anyone up here. I hoped you wouldn't come." That sounded cowardly, not to mention ungracious. "I mean I didn't want her to bother anyone on their day off."

He shrugged. "I drew the short straw. Ma said no one else was available. The insurance company will take care of damage, but I have to find a plumber to fix the original problem."

So he hadn't come on account of her. When disappointment tugged at her, she tried to replace it with an I'm-lucky-he-doesn't-care feeling that wouldn't quite take hold.

She watched him push open the door. "Brace yourself. Break out the life jackets. We're talking abandon ship. Women and children first." Fran handed him the card the insurance company had given her. "They removed the downstairs furniture and took it to storage."

He nodded. "Obviously they're doing cleanup now."

"Yeah. That motor belongs to the pump getting rid of the excess water," she explained. "Then they're going to lift the carpet and put fans around to dry it out before assessing what, if anything, can be salvaged."

He went inside to speak to the man in charge. Fran looked up at the sky and watched clouds roll in. The gusting wind was bitterly cold and she folded her arms over her chest against the chill. As soon as Alex came out, she would say goodbye and leave everything in his capable hands.

"They have everything under control," he said from the doorway behind her.

Fran turned, and his somber expression tugged at her heart. It was so different from how he'd looked when he'd told her about the cabin's romantic history. Obviously it held many happy memories. And now one not so happy.

She walked over to him and put her hand on his arm. "I'm sorry about this, Alex."

"We were lucky." He looked down at her. Between them, their mingled breath turned to a white cloud. He covered her fingers with his warm palm.

"You call that lucky?" she asked, angling her head toward where the crew was cleaning up.

He nodded. "Everyone in the family uses this place. And over the years we've established a list of things to do before leaving. The very last thing is shutting off the water. Someone forgot." He shook his head, and the breath he released was visible in the cold air. "It could have been a lot worse if you hadn't come up here."

She'd thought about that, too. "One of the guys said it's supposed to get even colder tonight. A storm's coming in, so it really could have been bad. I'm glad I could help."

"Me, too."

"So much for R and R." She saw her own breath as she sighed sadly. "I was looking forward to getting away. But now that you're here, I guess I'll head back down the mountain."

He frowned. "I'm only staying until the plumber gets here. When he fixes the sink there will be running water. The cleanup crew is almost finished. They're going to leave the fans going downstairs, but the second story where the bedrooms are is fine. There are separate heating units for each floor so it will be cozy and warm. You can still stay here. If you'd like."

She liked, and couldn't think of a single reason not to stay, since he was planning on driving back that night. She nodded. "Thanks, Alex. I think I will."

"Good." He glanced over his shoulder. "We're just in the way now. But since I am here, let me show you around town before I leave. It's the least I can do to apologize for the crisis."

"It's not your fault. No apology required."

"I insist."

Alex couldn't remember a luckier break or when apologizing had been so much fun. After his mother had called to tell him about the crisis, he'd suspected her of matchmaking again. But she'd insisted that he was the last one on her family list. Everyone else was tied up and couldn't go.

From the cabin, he'd called a plumber to fix the pipe. Then he and Fran had eaten a fast-food lunch. Now they were strolling along the main street of the Alpine village in the San Bernardino Mountains. Shop windows were filled with souvenirs and decorated with red hearts, white doilies and crimson crepe paper for Valentine's Day, just a little over a week away.

As they walked, their arms brushed or fingers touched, and each time he almost took her hand in his. But somehow, that felt more intimate than the kiss in her apartment. The meeting of mouths he could chalk up to pure and simple lust. But holding hands implied being a couple, which inferred being in love. That wasn't possible. Not a second time. When a Marchetti fell in love, it lasted a lifetime. At least that's what he'd told himself after Beth died.

But that was before he'd met Fran.

Now he wasn't so sure. He just knew there was a line between friendship and caring about someone that he didn't want to cross. Kissing her was easy to explain. He was a guy. He hadn't been able to help himself. But it was broad daylight now and they were in public. And the temptation of grabbing Fran's hand was almost more than he could resist. If only her shining eyes, full lips and easy laughter didn't grab him in the region of his heart. If only he didn't want to pull her into his arms and kiss her senseless—broad daylight and the curious public be damned.

"Let's go in here, Alex," she said, stopping in front of a card store.

"Okay." It would distract him, take the edge off his feelings.

The bell over the door tinkled as they went inside. In the front was a table of leftover Christmas decorations marked seventy-five percent off. The rest of the place had three dimensional red hearts and cupids festively displayed to draw the customer's attention to the one day of the year set aside for lovers. His brother's wedding day.

Alex envied Joe and Liz, and the rest of his siblings who had found contentment with someone. He and Luke were the only ones left. He couldn't speak for Luke, but Valentine's Day reminders made him wish a Marchetti got a second chance at love. The day set aside for lovers had a way of really making him feel alone.

Fran stopped at a stand of cards marked Wedding. "I need to get a card for Joe and Liz," she explained.

Had she been reading his mind? "You don't have to do that. I think helping with the food is enough," he answered.

"They were kind enough to ask me to be their guest as well. It's only polite to acknowledge their day."

"Even though the idea of marriage gives you a case of hives?"

She picked up a card and absently scanned the words. "Just because I don't want to fetch and carry for a man doesn't mean I don't believe it works for other people."

"I see." Funny, he'd sort of hoped she would say she'd changed her mind about marriage.

"Some people manage it successfully. Your sister, for instance. And your parents. And *my* parents, for goodness' sake. But after what I did at my mother's birthday, I guess you can see why it won't work for me." She slanted him a wry look. "I can't subject some poor unsuspecting guy to a milk shower just because he asks me to bring him something."

"Even if the poor unsuspecting guy knew what he was getting into? What if you fell head over heels in love?" he asked.

"That won't happen," she answered, turning away to put the card back.

Her response rankled. He told himself it had nothing to do with him. It was because she was made for love. He had tasted her passion and knew what a waste it would be if she turned her back on a relationship. If anyone knew how fulfilling it could be to love and be loved in return it was him. And he sensed that she had so much to give.

"How do you know?" he asked.

"How do I know what?"

"That you won't fall head over heels in love?"

"Because I won't let myself," she answered with absolute conviction.

Fran couldn't get the card-store conversation out of her mind for the rest of the day. In fact, the words came back in a more personal way as they were seated for dinner a little while later in a restaurant called Casual Elegance. A better name might have been the Love

Nest. Maybe all the Valentine hearts and cupids had put that thought in her head. To say nothing of the hunk and a half sitting across the table from her. But this place *was* perfect for lovers, she thought. And she couldn't help wondering if Alex had insisted that they come here because he'd taken her declaration to never fall in love as a personal challenge.

The quaint forest cottage, which they learned had been built in 1939, was like a country home. The forty-five seat restaurant was decorated with white lace curtains, colorful wreaths, dark wood furniture and glowing wall sconces. Classical music added an air of romantic sophistication.

The smiling hostess seated them and took their drink orders. The equally friendly server brought water, wine for her and a beer for him, and told them about the evening's specials. He discreetly drifted away when Alex informed him they needed a few minutes.

"So what do you think of the place?" he asked, looking around as if he already knew what she would say.

"This is exactly what I want my restaurant to be like someday," she answered.

"How do you know? You haven't tasted the food yet."

"It doesn't matter. In my own place, I can control the quality of what is served. But this quiet ambience is what I aspire to." She grinned. "Plus any restaurant that serves Baldamero dip—a creamy artichoke, spinach and Muenster cheese concoction—with sourdough toastettes as an appetizer is probably gonna be dynamite."

"You're right."

"Who'd have guessed there could be such an exceptional place tucked away here in the mountains?"

"Funny how we find what we've been looking for where we least expect it," he answered, catching and holding her gaze.

The intensity in his eyes made her heart race. She felt as if she was sliding out of control down an icy mountain, desperate for a handhold to stop her descent and prevent imminent danger and pain.

"Tell me about Beth," she blurted out.

She waited to see the shadow come over his face, but it never did. He calmly took his long-neck bottle of beer and lifted it to his mouth for a drink.

"What do you want to know?" he asked.

"What was it about her that you loved?" she asked simply.

He let out a long breath. "Why don't you ask me the atomic weight of Denver?" he said. "That would be easier to answer."

"Then tell me what you miss," she suggested.

He thought for a few moments. "Her unselfishness. She was such a giving person. Always doing for me without complaint or expecting anything in return."

"She sounds like a saint, or my mother. Come to think of it, my mother is a saint." Unlike me, she thought, feeling uncomfortable somehow. "What did she look like?" she asked, almost afraid to hear the answer.

Without hesitation, Alex said, "An angel. Her hair was golden-blond, eyes as blue as the unpolluted sky here in the mountains. And tall, almost my height," he finished.

Completely different from me, Fran thought, somehow feeling deflated.

"Can I ask you another question?"

"If I said no, would it stop you?" he asked, his mouth turning up at the corners.

"Probably not." She couldn't return his smile. "Why did you want to know how I know that I won't fall head over heels in love?"

"Because, in my experience, it isn't something you can prevent. It just happens. And I just don't picture you as the type to be alone for the rest of your life."

"But you saw for yourself how my family is. The way my mother takes care of everyone else and has lost herself. I've just figured out who I am."

"No one can take that away from you," he answered.

"Not consciously. But it would happen just the same. Why would I want to change?"

"I don't see that falling in love has to change you," he answered.

She narrowed her eyes at him. "Why are you trying to talk me into something I've been successfully avoiding for a long time?"

"I just think you're made for love."

"Well, you're wrong."

"Have you ever been in love?"

"I thought I was. The guy in cooking school," she reminded him. At his nod she continued. "But that wasn't even close."

"Then you don't know what you're missing."

She frowned. "Look, just because you sign my paycheck doesn't give you the right to run my life."

"I wasn't trying—"

"Yes, you were. And here's food for thought—if *you* can prevent yourself from falling in love again, why can't I keep it from happening in the first place?"

She let the statement hang there for a moment, then added, "In fact, it's easier for me. I don't have anything to compare it to."

To her surprise, Alex just smiled at her. "See, it's that passionate nature of yours that convinces me you need love."

She stared at him for a few moments, then burst out laughing. "You're impossible."

"It's my best quality," he said, grinning.

"Remind me to quarantine you from Valentine's Day displays." Ditto for herself. She kept a firm grip on her heart as she let her gaze wander over his dark hair and smoldering eyes, the masculine shadow of beard on his cheeks and jaw. "You don't look a thing like cupid."

"No, but—"

She held up her hand. "I'm changing the subject now," she announced.

"To what?" he asked.

She looked out the window. "To that," she said, pointing. "I'm a southern California girl born and raised. But even I recognize that the white stuff falling from the sky is snow."

He lifted the lace curtain beside him and frowned. "If that keeps up, it means we're stuck with each other in the cabin tonight."

"Stuck?" She raised one eyebrow. "An interesting choice of words."

"It's too dangerous to drive down the mountain in weather like this. Do you mind if I stay over with you?"

Of course she minded. "It's your place," she said, hoping her shrug had just the right amount of casual.

"I can't very well ask you to leave." Even she heard the edgy note in her voice.

"Are you afraid to stay with me?" His gaze settled on her mouth and, if possible, grew more intense.

"Why would I be?" she asked.

"Because I kissed you."

She groaned inwardly. Why did he have to bring that up? What had made him think of it? She thought they'd managed to get past the earth-moving experience without having to talk about it. "I'd forgotten all about that."

His laugh told her he knew she was lying. "Okay, we'll play by your rules. We'll forget about kissing."

"So which bedroom do you want me in?" Fran asked.

"Mine," Alex answered, without missing a beat.

She whirled around and stared at him. Speechless, she felt her eyes widen.

"Did I really say that out loud?" he asked. "I was kidding."

"You don't look like you're kidding." Before he could mask his expression, she'd seen hungry longing on his face.

They were standing in the upstairs loft surveying doors number one, two and three. The open area was like a grownup male playroom. A pool table dominated the center of the space and on the wall beside it was a rack for the cues. The opposite wall held a dartboard. Leather sofas with hunter-green throws across the back rimmed the perimeter. There was a low hum from the fans still running downstairs. But the second floor was toasty warm and getting hotter by the second.

He had told her that this cabin was where several

members of his family had fallen in love. He had told her he wasn't looking for love. She'd counted on that. Now this Freudian slip about his bedroom. Could the icy road down the mountain be any more slippery than the situation she found herself in now?

"Even if I wasn't kidding, what are you afraid of, Fran?"

"Myself." She leaned back against the pool table and folded her arms across her chest. "I'm going to go out on a limb here, Alex. I don't know if you feel it or not, but there's this really annoying attraction sort of thing going on with us."

He set her small suitcase down and moved in front of her. "Yeah. I sort of felt it. I've been out of circulation awhile, but I'm still breathing," he said wryly.

"Awhile? Does that mean you are officially looking for a woman now?" Her heart pounded like the bass drum in the New Year's Day parade.

"No." He shook his head emphatically. "It means I think we should explore this annoying attraction. If we get it out in the open, deal with it, then we can let it go."

He took a step closer. The wonderful masculine scent of his cologne surrounded her. The heat from his body reached out to her, drawing her to him. Her will to resist was stretched to the breaking point.

"Define explore," she said breathlessly.

"I'll demonstrate explore, but first I need to warn you that I did in fact agree to your rule. But my heart wasn't in it."

Before she could ask which rule he meant, he reached out and took her face in his hands, then bent slightly to touch his lips to hers. The contact made her stomach drop as if she were riding a white-knuckle ride at an amusement park. Her heart hammered against the wall of her chest. He tunneled his fingers into her loose hair as he slowly, thoroughly, tenderly caressed her mouth.

As if they had a mind of their own, her arms uncrossed and she rested her hands on his chest. He settled his hand at her waist, drawing her to him. Fran's breath caught as her resistance melted away. She relished the sensation of his other arm pulling her still closer and holding her tight. She was intoxicated by the mingling warmth of their bodies on a cold night, the way his kiss made her tingle from head to toe.

It had been *so* long since she'd been held like this. No. She'd been in a man's arms before, but she'd never been held quite this way. Or maybe it was the fact that Alex was the only man who had ever made her feel so deeply. The emotion, whatever it was, was so profound that it frightened her. It made her wonder "what if." That was a dangerous game to play.

But she couldn't resist participating just a little longer. Beyond the circle of his embrace was a cold, lonely existence, and she wasn't ready to go back there just yet.

Fran slid her arms up his chest, reveling in the restrained power there. She pressed closer and heard his quick intake of breath. A small smile curved her lips and he felt it.

"Two can play at this," he said, his voice hoarse and his breathing ragged. "Like arm wrestling, a sneak attack is the way to achieve one's objective."

"And what's your goal?" she whispered against his lips.

"I'll show you."

He nibbled the corner of her mouth, the curve of her

jaw, then the underside, moving steadily toward her neck. When he pressed a kiss there, a lovely little spot just in the hollow beneath her ear, Fran couldn't hold back a moan of pleasure.

"Mission accomplished," he mumbled.

His mouth continued a delicious assault on her throat and the results turned her insides to liquid honey. Her chest rose and fell rapidly, and still she couldn't seem to draw enough air into her lungs. Certainly it was the altitude in the mountains and the lack of oxygen that was causing her to behave this way. It was crazy. He seemed to have a power over her. Was it love?

Lord, she hoped not. She refused to let it be. It was a no-win situation because he could never love her back. And if he did, she would lose herself.

She pulled back and lowered her arms to his shoulders. "We can't do this, Alex."

He blinked and looked at her with a dazed expression. "I thought we were pulling it off rather well." His own breathing was ragged and fast.

"Way too well," she agreed, stepping out of the circle of his arms.

Without the warmth of his body surrounding her, cold enveloped her. She shivered, and he tried to pull her back against him.

"No," she said. "We have to forget this ever happened."

He ran a shaking hand through his hair. "Short of a blow on the head resulting in amnesia, I think that's an impossible assignment."

"I mean it. This is a recipe for disaster. We work together. Mixing business with..."

"*Pleasure* is the word you're looking for," he supplied.

"Whatever you want to call it, we're asking for trouble if we don't stop. Remember the project? Making the family proud?"

He drew in a shuddering breath. "I fail to see what one has to do with the other."

"At the risk of beating a dead horse, we've already established that you're not looking for love and neither am I. No matter how civilized we think we are, this can only end badly. What about the project then?"

He didn't say anything for several moments. He just stared at her with a dark, intense yearning. She thought he would tug her back into his arms. She almost wished he would.

Finally he said, "I suppose you're right. This isn't a good idea."

Fran felt a sharp pain in the region of her heart. She'd been hurt once before by a man who'd cozied up to her for his own career. Now she and Alex had agreed to turn off the heat for the sake of both their careers.

Surely it was for the best? Since when did being right, or doing what was for the best, hurt so much?

"You take the bedroom at the far end of the hall. That was Rosie's. It's decorated girly." He let out a long breath. "I'll take the one at the top of the stairs."

That left a whole bedroom between them. Not nearly enough real estate to take the heat off and bring her thermostat down to normal. Fran glanced out the window and saw that the snow was coming down heavier in huge, white, fluffy flakes. Unfortunately, that small amount of square footage would have to do.

She nodded. "Good night, Alex."

If only it could be goodbye to cabin, boss, job, her heart would stay in one functional piece. But she still had four weeks left on her contract. Not to mention that she'd agreed to do the food for his brother's wedding.

When that obligation was over, no more socializing outside of work.

"Good night, Fran."

He disappeared into his room, but the deep, masculine sound of his voice made her want to march up to that closed door and beg for entrance. And how was that different from the way she felt about him at the office?

She sighed. It was going to be a very long four weeks.

Chapter Ten

Joe Marchetti's wedding to Liz Anderson had gone off without a hitch. Well, maybe one. They were now hitched, as in man and wife, Fran noted with a small smile.

The ceremony had been lovely. In deference to Valentine's Day the color scheme was red and white. The groom was handsome in his less formal than a tuxedo black suit, cream shirt and red tie. The bride was radiantly lovely in a floor-length, long-sleeved white chiffon gown. Her pretty maid of honor, Samantha Taylor, wore a long red velvet dress.

Dinner had gone off without a hitch, too. Fran had breathed a sigh of relief when the bride and groom had thanked her. The food had been as big a success as everything else. In the corporate kitchen, she had prepared chicken, fish and beef entrées and all the trimmings, then it had been transported to Flo and Tom Marchetti's home for the small affair. It was a weeknight because of the newlywed couple's determination to have their anniversary on Valentine's Day. Such an achingly romantic gesture.

Fran groaned inwardly. Until she'd grown up and grown cynical, she'd had a special someone for her valentine every time the day rolled around. Joe had paired her with Alex at the wedding, but she wouldn't let him be special to her. It would hurt too much on February 15, when she was alone again.

If she could get through this entire day set apart for lovers and not do anything stupid, like fall in love, she would be a happy girl. In the mountains a week ago, she'd accused Alex of being susceptible to the suggestion of Valentine's Day. Now here they were at ground zero, and what could be more magical than a wedding? But so far Alex had been polite, yet reserved. And, hard as she'd tried, she couldn't seem to suppress the disappointment she felt at his indifference.

The Marchettis home was a one-story, rambling California ranch style. There was a whole lot of square footage, and whenever Fran had to go anywhere by herself, she resisted the urge to drop a trail of bread crumbs in order to find her way back. The tastefully decorated rooms were done in shades of beige, hunter green and coral. For the reception, they had moved the chocolate-colored leather sofas out of the family room and set up four circular tables that would each seat ten people.

Except for the food, Flo Marchetti had arranged everything: the white tablecloths with red overlaid linen; red and white roses, carnations and baby's breath for the centerpieces. Floral arrangements sat in every corner of the house, and the fragrant perfume of the blossoms filled the air. A three-tiered wedding cake, surrounded by flowers, sat on a table.

The seating had presumably been arranged by the groom's mother, and Fran and Alex had eaten together with a good portion of the Marchetti family at their table. But he had disappeared, excusing himself for pictures or something. It was probably the truth, since the rest of their dinner companions vanished, too. Fran rested her chin on her palm.

Then Flo Marchetti materialized beside her. "I'm sorry we deserted you. Pushy photographer. Mind if I join you? I've been wanting to talk to you all evening."

"Please." She held out her hand, wondering what the woman wanted to talk about. Duh. Fran realized she wouldn't be winning any prizes for intelligence. Of course the woman was dying to discuss Alex.

"I just wanted to thank you for everything you did. The food was wonderful."

Fran smiled. "You're welcome. I'm glad you enjoyed it."

"Not just me. Everyone is raving. And not only about the entrées. They want to know who the babe is. You look lovely, Fran." The other woman studied her from head to toe. "That dress is very becoming. I like the shades of cream and beige together, not to mention the flattering style."

"Thanks." The sleeveless sheath topped by a matching coat with cream lapels was new, but Fran wasn't about to share the information. She didn't want Alex's mother to read anything into it, like that Fran wanted to look her best to impress his family. Even though that was true.

Flo Marchetti had to be in her late fifties, but could easily pass for ten years younger. She was trim and at least five or six inches taller than Fran, which made her glad they were sitting down. The other woman's short, silver hair was fashionably styled, with wisps framing her relatively unlined face.

Fran tucked a strand of hair behind her ear. "You look terrific, too," she said sincerely. "Your dress is also very becoming."

"How nice of you to say that." Flo glanced down at her floor-length, peach-colored, two-piece suit. "At the rate my children are getting married, I'm going to have a closetful of dresses that I can't ever wear again."

"I can tell that you're just hating every minute of this wedding," Fran commented wryly.

The other woman grinned. "I couldn't be happier. And truthfully, I didn't have to buy a dress for Rosie's wedding. She and Steve married in Reno."

"I didn't know she eloped," Fran said.

"It wasn't an elopement, exactly. You'll have to ask her to tell you the story sometime. It's very romantic."

"I will."

"Three down, two to go," the older woman sighed.

Fran laughed politely, but the words tugged at her heart. She looked at the other woman's radiant face. Did she know that Alex was never going to marry?

"Did you and Alex have a nice time at the cabin? We were in the middle of wedding plans, and Alex was the only one available to go to your rescue."

Fran studied her for signs of fibbing. Nick had been best man tonight, but it was on the tip of her tongue to demand what had made Luke too busy to bail her out. Literally. Common sense prevailed and she struggled to keep her expression bland. Nice wasn't quite the adjective she would use to describe their time at the cabin. Frustrating would be more accurate. Knowing he was *there*, but she couldn't touch him the way she wanted, or be with him the way he'd made her need, was her hell on earth. Thank God the roads were safe the next day and she'd been able to leave. Leave? Full retreat was more like it.

"The mountains were wonderful," Fran answered. "In spite of the flood, the cabin was a relaxing change of scene."

Liar, liar, pants on fire, she thought. No wonder she was being punished with hell on earth.

"Okay. I won't embarrass you further by asking for details." Flo's gaze narrowed. "But can we talk about your negotiating technique with my son?"

"The kiss?" Fran's gaze snapped to the other woman's. She didn't look upset, annoyed or anything other than the pleased mother of the groom.

"That's the one. A humdinger, too. And a stroke of genius."

"It was?"

"Absolutely. You persuaded him to your way of thinking without ranting and raving. Or pouting. Ingenious way to handle your boss. But risky."

Fran nodded. "A calculated risk. I've never worked for a man more fair and reasonable than Alex."

Not to mention cute, sexy and just plain exciting.

"Does he know you're in love with him?"

Fran was just taking a sip from her water glass and sucked in air at the same time. She started to choke. The other woman patted her on the back.

When Fran could speak, she said, "I have to request that you never again say something so controversial when I'm drinking."

"Controversial? In what way?"

Fran shook her head. "Implying that we have anything besides a mutually satisfying working relationship,'' she said coolly. But her pulse pounded a mile a minute.

"I'm his mother, Fran. You can tell me what's going on with you and my son.''

"Nothing's going on. Really,'' she protested.

"But you'd like there to be?''

"No,'' Fran disagreed. "Yes. Maybe.'' She was so confused. And why on God's green earth was she sharing her bewilderment with Alex's mother, of all people? Time for some serious damage control. "It doesn't matter what I'm feeling—or not feeling. Alex has been completely up front and honest about everything. He told me about Beth.''

Flo's brown eyes narrowed as her mouth pulled tight for a moment. "Yes. Beth.''

"What?''

"Oh, nothing,'' she said quickly, cautiously. "She was a lovely girl. So tragic that she and Alex didn't have the opportunity to let their relationship play out naturally.''

An odd way to put it, Fran thought. "What was she like?''

"Beautiful. A kindergarten teacher. She wanted to be a wife and mother—a homemaker. She was very giving of herself. Catered to Alex shamelessly.''

Fran would have sworn that his mother didn't approve of her son's former fiancée. "Is that a bad thing?''

"No.'' But she didn't sound convinced. "Maybe just a little too selfless at times.''

"I don't see how that's—''

"Excuse me, Fran dear. I'm getting the high sign from my husband. It could mean one of two things.

Mind my own business, or Joe and Liz are getting ready to cut the cake.''

"My money is on cake cutting," Fran said as she watched the happy couple take their places beside the three-tiered concoction.

Flo smiled and patted her hand. "I've enjoyed talking with you. Can we pick up the conversation later?" At Fran's nod, the other woman impulsively hugged her, then stood and joined the other family members.

Alex was like a homing device for Fran's gaze. She always seemed to zero in on him with little effort or conscious thought. Now he was smiling and laughing with his brothers and sister. He looked so handsome that her breath caught and stuck in her chest. He was the best looking of the Marchetti men by far. In his dark suit with the satiny charcoal shirt and matching tie, he had an air of bad boy about him that made her heart beat faster. There was a rascally quality that she'd never seen before. Her legs felt weak, like underwhipped meringue. If she'd been standing, there would have been an embarrassingly loud thud when she hit the floor.

Was his mother right? Was she in love with him? Did she want him to return her feelings?

But she was so not his type. Beth had been tall and blond and saintly. Fran was short, brunette and so not saintly. She was the polar opposite of the woman Alex had loved. What kind of chance did she have with him?

She was twenty-five years old, and had reached her adult height a long time ago. Although she could lighten her hair color, it probably wouldn't complement her skin tone. The only thing she had control over was attitude. She could be selfless and giving if she really tried—and had a really good reason. Scratch that. She could give it a try, say for twenty-four hours, just to see if it might work.

When family pictures were finally over, Alex looked for Fran and found her cutting the cake. Joe and Liz had done the traditional thing, and Fran was taking over now. Servers hired for the evening were distributing the dessert to the guests.

He sat down and put his jacket over the chair next to his, reserving it for Fran. Even though Joe had suggested they pair off for the wedding, Alex didn't think of this as a date. The thought made him a little sad. More than any other day, this one set aside for lovers made him miss having someone—to buy cards, flowers and candy for.

Before he had time for sadness to sink in, there was a piece of cake in front of him. Expecting to see one of the servers, he looked up and was pleased that Fran stood there. "Thanks."

"You're welcome. Would you like some coffee?"

"Sounds good. Why don't you join me—" Before he could get the words out, she had picked up his cup and saucer and turned away. She waylaid one of the servers, who poured steaming coffee into the cup.

"Here you go," she said, then sat down beside him.

"Thanks." He looked around the table for cream and sugar.

"Sorry. I forgot you take stuff in it."

Instantly she reached for the matching silver condiment containers. Then she put in a teaspoon of sugar and tilted the creamer spout until just a couple drops of half-and-half lightened the dark liquid. Just the way he liked it.

That was surprise enough, her remembering the exact way he took his coffee. But he found himself speechless at this solicitous Fran. Maybe she'd been abducted by aliens and a three-dimensional hologram left in her place.

"There you go," she said, sliding his cup toward him.

"Thanks." He took a sip. "Perfect."

"We aim to please. And give," she added, smiling sweetly.

"Okay," he said skeptically. If she batted her eyelashes at him, he was outta there. This was a side of Fran Carlino he'd never seen before. He wasn't altogether sure he liked it. "What were you and my mother talking about?"

She looked uncomfortable for a moment, as if she was censoring herself. "Oh, just food, flowers, fashion," she said breezily.

"Really? You looked awfully serious."

"You were watching me?" The corners of her full mouth turned up as if the idea of him searching her out gave her pleasure.

"Of course. You are my d—" He'd been about to say "date." But that's not what they were. "Dinner partner."

"I see," she said. "And along with polite conversation, you have the sacred duty to keep an eye on me for the evening?" she asked, a snap to her voice.

There was a spark of the Fran he knew and... Loved?

No. He was a Marchetti. Love came along only once in a lifetime.

Thoughts of Beth came to mind—her constant eagerness to please. He suddenly realized that he hadn't missed her, not for a long time. She would always have a place in his heart, but she didn't have a lock on it anymore.

He looked at Fran. Now if he could just figure out what she was up to. "Would you like to see the back-yard?"

She thought for a moment, then smiled. "Yes. I was so busy when I got here that I didn't get the outside tour."

He stood up and grabbed his coat from the back of her chair. "Follow me."

She saluted. "I hear and obey, fearless leader."

He rolled his eyes, then led her out of the family room, through the kitchen where the serving staff was cleaning up, and out the back door.

"This is the patio and pool area," he explained. "There's grass out there."

"It's lovely." She looked up at the star-filled sky and drew in a deep breath. "And what a beautiful night." Then she shivered.

"You're cold," he said, dragging his coat around her shoulders.

"Thanks." Leaning back against the wooden beam supporting the patio cover, she gripped the lapels of his jacket and drew in another deep breath as a small, sat-isfied smile teased her lips.

"What did you think of the wedding?" he asked. He moved close to her and rested a hand on the post, above her head.

"Beautiful. Everything was perfect."

"So what were you and my mother really talking about?" he asked again.

She hesitated a moment before saying, "You. Among other things."

"Oh boy. What did Flo say?"

"She approved of my negotiating technique."

The family test tasting. The kiss that had launched a thousand feelings—not to mention giving him ideas now. Don't go there, he cautioned himself. He'd barely managed to spend the night with her at the cabin and not taste her lips again. And in the days that followed, she had been on his mind twenty-four hours a day. Even in his dreams, she taunted him, with the memory of her breasts burning into his chest. But every time he awoke, his arms were empty and the place in the bed beside him was cold. But he was never cold when Fran was nearby.

"What else did my mother say?" he asked, yanking his thoughts back to the present. At Fran's skeptical look, he added, "You two were talking for a while."

"Oh, lots of things," she said vaguely. Then an anxious expression replaced the dreamy look in her eyes. "You left your cake. I'll go inside and get it for you."

Alex suddenly felt the cold. What was going on? Where was the Fran who would just as soon make him wear the cake as deliver it to him? What had happened to the spirited chef who had railed against fetching and carrying for a man? Where was the woman who had gotten his attention when she'd sworn never to throw her hat in the fetching-and-carrying ring by telling a man "I do"?

He lowered his arm and backed away from her. What the hell had made him think of marrying her, anyway?

"Don't bother," he said. "It's time to go back inside."

Chapter Eleven

"I'm in trouble, Ma."

The words were out of Fran's mouth before she closed the door to her parents' home. It was the day after the wedding. Unable to concentrate, she'd left work about an hour early without saying goodbye to Alex. She couldn't face him. His dumbfounded expression following her offer to drop off his dry cleaning had been too humiliating. Hence her motivation for stopping by to see her mother.

"You're *in* trouble?" Aurora asked, her brown eyes widening.

"Not *that*. Trouble of the confusion kind," she clarified.

Her mother put her arm around Fran's shoulders and led her into the kitchen. "Have a seat and tell me all about it while I fix you a snack. You need strength for girl talk."

Fran pulled out one of the wooden ladder-back

chairs at the table and released a sigh when she settled herself on the floral-print cushion. "It's about Alex."

"Tell me something I don't know," Aurora said as she set a plate of cookies and a glass of milk in front of her daughter. "You're in love with him. I just don't understand why you would think that's trouble."

"I'm not in love with him." At least she hoped not. Because she was afraid he couldn't love her back. "My worst fear has become a reality. I've turned into a Stepford woman. Scraping and bowing until I want to gag. I offered to drop off his cleaning, Ma."

Aurora sat down across from her with a freshly washed bunch of grapes, a paper towel and a pair of scissors. As she listened, she cut the large clump into neat little clusters and arranged them on the plate, settling them beside the cookies.

"You're going to have to be more specific, Frannie."

Sighing loudly, Fran took a cookie and bit into it as she organized her thoughts. "Alex is in love with another woman."

"No," her mother gasped. "The two-timing son of a—"

"Ma!" Fran laughed in spite of her inner turmoil. "It was a long time ago and she passed away. But he hasn't gotten over her."

"Oh, that's very sad. But what does that have to do with his cleaning?"

"I'm nothing like her. Beth was perfect. She was an angel, even looked like one. Tall, golden hair, blue eyes."

Her mother stood and went to the silverware drawer for a fork, spoon and knife. Then she grabbed a napkin and folded it in half, the diagonal way that made triangles. She set it beside Fran's plate before settling across from her again.

"How do you know that's what angels look like?" she asked.

"Aside from the fact that I'm short, dumpy and have mousy brown hair, that's not really the point, Ma. I'm talking about what she was."

"And what was she?"

"Like I said, a perfect human being."

"There's no such thing, although women come very close."

Fran sighed as she finished her cookie and took a small cluster of grapes. "If Alex was here, I'd be peeling them for him because that's what she would have done. She was a kindergarten teacher. All she wanted was to be a wife and mother. Alex adored her. I'm the complete opposite. From the moment I met him, I've done nothing but tell him that I'm a career woman. That in my book marriage is nothing more than servitude."

Her mother stood up. "I forgot. I have some of that cheese you like, and the little crackers to put it on."

Fran stared at her mother. The woman hadn't sat for more than thirty seconds since she'd arrived. Come to think of it, she always did this. And not just for her husband. Fran had seen her mother cater and fuss for Max, Mike, Sam and Johnny. And her, too.

"Ma, what are you doing?"

"I told you. I'm getting you some of that good jalapeño and pepper cheese you like."

Fran shook her head. "No. I mean you don't have to wait on me." She pointed to the plate. "There's enough here to feed me for the rest of the day. If I want anything else, I can stand up and get it."

Aurora smiled. "Of course you can. But I like doing it for you, sweetheart."

"But I don't want to make more work for you."

"I love you," her mother said simply. "It's not a chore when you love someone."

"And that's why you fetch and carry for Daddy? You don't feel like a servant?"

Aurora laughed. "Of course not. But he works hard. I love him very much and he feels the same. I enjoy making his life a little easier when he's home. It's my job. Like you cook gourmet food. But if I didn't want to do it, no force on this earth could make me. I'm a very lucky woman."

Fran stared as thoughts tumbled through her head. She'd always known that her parents loved each other and her. But still she'd chafed at her mother's indulging her father. Fran had never stopped to realize that her mother treated everyone she cared about the same way.

"I never thought about it like that," Fran admitted. That realization called for another homemade cookie.

Aurora brought the container to the table and sat down as she refilled the plate. "It's no secret that your father wants you to marry and have babies. For that matter, so do I—if you fall in love."

There was no "if" about it. Fran knew she was in love with her boss. For all the good it would do her. Her chances of a happy ending with Alex were slim to none.

Her mother took a clump of grapes. "But neither of us wants you to give up yourself for a man. Things will fall into place if you're happy with who you are."

"Did it happen that way for you, Ma?"

Aurora nodded. "I'm a homemaker by choice. But

there's a small part of me that wonders what it would have been like to have it all. A family *and* a career. You'll have that.''

"I don't think so, Ma."

Fran knew no other man would make her feel the way Alex did. And he'd already lost his heart to someone else. Still, she'd fallen for him like a ton of bricks. All her self-protection had been about as helpful as an umbrella in a nuclear blast.

The front door opened and her father called out, "I'm home." Then he appeared in the kitchen doorway. "This is a pleasant surprise. My two favorite ladies." He leaned over and kissed Fran on the forehead. Then he walked around the table, pulled his wife to her feet and into his arms before kissing her soundly on the mouth.

Fran smiled fondly at them, then cleared her throat. "Maybe you guys should get a room."

"You might have something there," Leo said, winking at her. "This is what I want for you, Frannie."

"What, Dad?" she asked.

"A man who will love you like I love your mother. Someone to share your life with, because a job isn't everything. All it does is put a roof over your head and food on the table."

"Even if it is just frozen food," she said with a sigh.

"Don't knock it. Four billion dollars a year is a lot of linguine. I don't need to get baptized with a glass of milk to see the forest for the trees."

Fran smiled at his mixed metaphor, then frowned as the message sank in. "Daddy, I just want you to be proud of me—to love me—like you do the boys."

Leo met her gaze and there was a serious look on his weathered face. With his arm around his wife's waist, he studied her. "You really don't have any idea how proud I am of my little girl? You don't know how much I love you?"

The words warmed her heart, but she said, "No. Tell me."

"Your mother explained some things to me, kiddo. I know I wasn't very supportive when you went to cooking school. In spite of that, you went after what you wanted with Carlino determination. More than I've ever seen from your brothers. I guess I was so busy telling you what to do that I forgot to tell you how much I admire the way you do it. Don't ever doubt that I love you very much. I just want you to be safe. And happy. Like I am with this woman here."

He bent Aurora back over his arm and kissed her passionately again. When they straightened, her mother blushed like a schoolgirl and her father's laugh was lusty and filled with love.

Suddenly Fran understood everything. Her dad wasn't against her career, he just wanted her to find the lifetime of happiness that he and her mother had. In his guy-way he'd made it all about her being safe and secure so he wouldn't have to worry about her. But fetching and carrying wasn't about servitude. It was about love.

She stood up and rounded the table to where the two stood in each other's arms. "Group hug," she said.

Leo Carlino swung one arm wide and pulled her into the circle of his embrace. He kissed the top of her head. "I love you, sweet pea."

"I love you, too, Dad."

She loved Alex as well. But she realized she couldn't change for him. It wasn't fair to him. Mostly it wasn't fair to her. And she intended to tell him so.

* * *

Alex looked at the clock on his desk, which said six o'clock. Leaving at this time of evening would put him in the middle of rush hour traffic. He was going to be at least twenty minutes late picking up his mother for dinner. His father had gone to a hockey game with Luke. When Alex had found out Flo would be alone, he'd asked her out.

He stood up and grabbed his suit coat from the back of his chair. When he turned around, he saw Fran in the doorway.

Ever since her talk with his mother last night, Fran had turned schizophrenic. He wondered which of her personalities had shown up now—Xena Warrior Princess, who stirred his blood with something he shied away from naming, or Susie Homemaker, who made him nervous as a long-tailed cat in a room full of rocking chairs.

"Hi," he said, slipping his jacket on.

"Are you on your way out?" she asked.

"Yes. I've got a date with—"

"This can wait," she interrupted. She turned away. "Bye."

"No." He walked across the room and grabbed the door before she could close it. They were alone in the office. His secretary and the rest of the staff had left for the evening. "I've got a minute. What can I do for you?"

She stood in the doorway with her arms crossed over her chest. The vulnerability he saw in her expression pulled at his heart, and he wanted to fold her in his arms. He wanted to protect her from whatever was causing it. He wanted to take care of her in spite of the kowtowing of the last twenty-four hours. Her behavior had bothered him. That wasn't the spirited Fran he knew and... Yes, loved.

"I don't want to hold you up," she said.

"You're not. What is it?"

She met his gaze. "I've only got about three weeks left on my contract."

"I know. We need to talk—"

"I just wanted to remind you that I'll need a letter of recommendation."

"What?" Surprise slammed him in the chest and drove the air from his lungs.

"It's time for me to think about my next job. I would like a letter of recommendation. The main reason I took this assignment was for experience in entrées for my résumé. I've got that now."

"You're going to quit?"

"I'm not resigning. My contract is almost up."

"What if I want to renew it?"

"The answer would have to be no."

"Why?"

"Oh, you know. The usual," she said nonchalantly, with a too-casual shrug.

"So you're unhappy here?"

She shook her head. "It's been a wonderful experience working with you and your staff."

Another thought occurred to him. "Have you already had an offer from one of our competitors?"

"No." She laughed. "But from your mouth to God's ear."

"If it's a raise—"

She shook her head. "The compensation is more than generous."

"Then give me an opportunity to renegotiate your contract."

"No," she said sharply.

"Why? Did a position at the grill and taco bar open up? For that matter, what's come over you lately?"

Her eyes flashed and an angry flush crept into her cheeks. This glimmer of her usual spirit made him want to pump his arm and shout, "Yes!"

"If you must know, I don't want to renew my contract because I don't fit in here."

"What are you talking about?"

"I cheat at arm wrestling. I'm likely to dump milk on you. I say what I think, and I don't cater, as in humor, cosset, coddle or indulge. I can't change the way I am. For the last twenty-four hours I tried, and I hated it, myself and you. Even if I could change, I wouldn't. For you or any other man—boss," she amended.

"I never asked you to change."

After he'd spoken, Alex didn't understand the devastation that haunted her eyes. She couldn't change; he didn't want her to. Simple. Then why did she look as if he'd just put too much pepper into her signature recipe?

Before she whirled around, he could have sworn he saw the sheen of tears in her eyes. But when she spoke, her voice was steady and firm. "Good. Then we have nothing more to say. I'll fulfill the terms of my contract and you'll prepare a letter of recommendation."

"I'll have my secretary type it up first thing tomorrow."

She was gone before Alex could collect his thoughts. He was alone before he could plead with her to stay, to not abandon him. But something had stopped him.

A voice inside said if he did, he was crossing a line and could never go back. So he said nothing.

He'd never had her in the first place, but his heart ached as if she was lost to him forever.

Chapter Twelve

"**I**'m a blockhead?"

Angry, Alex stared at his mother across the linen-covered, flower-and-candle-bedecked table in the very expensive restaurant he'd taken her to. He had hoped she could lift his spirits. Instead of a mother lion defending her cub, she'd thrown him to the wolves.

"It hurts me to say it more than it hurts you to hear it," she said sympathetically.

Alex doubted that very much. He had explained to Flo what had happened with his favorite little frozen food chef to make him late for dinner. And she'd responded by calling him names.

"Okay. What have I done that justifies you calling me a blockhead?"

"It's what you didn't do," she began, in that patient, patronizing tone. "You should have pleaded with her to stay instead of agreeing so quickly to give in to her request for a letter of recommendation."

"I told her I wanted to renegotiate, but she turned me down flat."

"Did she give you any explanation?"

"She said she wasn't going to change for any man." His mother's gaze skittered away for a moment. "Uh-oh."

"I don't like the sound of that." His stomach clenched. Two wordlets, one syllable each that sent dread coursing through him. What the hell did "uh-oh" mean? It was the first inkling he'd had that he'd confided in his mother hoping she would reassure him that Fran hadn't meant what she'd said and it would all blow over.

"What does that mean?" he asked.

His mother frowned, then took a sip of her white wine. "It would appear that the fruit doesn't fall far from the tree. And any tendency you have toward being a blockhead was inherited from me."

"You want to explain that?" he asked, frowning in bewilderment.

"I'm afraid it's my fault that Fran wants to leave."

He really didn't like hearing "Fran" and "leave" in the same sentence. "How's that?" he asked in as calm a tone as he could manage.

"She's in love with you," Flo said simply.

Fran was in love with him? Miss "Love, marriage, and servitude go hand in hand"? The idea made his heart pound in a dance of joy and exultation. But he couldn't quite believe it. Or maybe he didn't want to? If he did, he would have to admit what he felt for her.

"Ma, start at the beginning. You lost me back at the part where you knocked your own gene pool."

Flo took a piece of dark bread from the cloth-covered basket on the table and set it on her plate. As she looked at him, she started pulling off little pieces. "I made it a point to talk to Fran at the wedding. To thank her for doing such a wonderful job with the food," she added.

"And?" he prodded. She was the mother of all matchmakers and must have had another motive besides that.

"I could see that there was something going on between the two of you."

"Okay. Now we're getting somewhere."

"She asked me what Beth was like."

Alex remembered her asking him, too. At the cabin. "What did you tell her?"

"The truth. That Beth catered to you shamelessly and was just a little too selfless."

"What does that mean, Ma?"

"Come on, Alex. Now you're being worse than a blockhead. And dense doesn't become you. I don't like to speak ill of the dead, but Beth practically cut your meat for you. She was a sweet girl, and what happened was tragic. I'd give almost anything to have prevented what happened to her—and to you. But we all felt like pond scum around her."

"Pond scum?" he asked, but somehow he knew what she was going to say.

"Yes. The whole family. She made us all feel inadequate. There was just something about her we felt was wrong for you."

"Why didn't anyone mention this to me?" He knew what his mother meant. He'd felt it himself, but had chosen to ignore the doubts. He remembered trying to give to Beth and always feeling as if it wasn't enough.

Flo sighed. "You would have become defensive. Your father and I talked about it endlessly and were just grateful that you had the good sense to put off marriage. I have something to ask you and I don't mean for you to give me an answer. But really think about it.''

''What, Ma?''

''Would Beth really have made you happy?'' She held up her hand. ''Don't say anything.''

He nodded. ''But I think I know what you're getting at.''

He did. It was suddenly crystal clear.

''There's more,'' his mother said. ''About Fran, I mean.''

If she kept this up, he would be in so deep, he could never dig his way out. ''Let me have it.''

''I told Fran she was very different from Beth. But I meant it in a good way.'' His mother's attractive face filled with regret and concern. ''I didn't get an opportunity to add that the differences were refreshing and wonderful. That I hadn't seen you look so happy and so…alive for a very long time.''

Bingo. That was why she'd taken to scraping and bowing in the middle of the reception. And it explained the cream and sugar in his coffee, the offer to fetch his cake and drop off his dry cleaning. She was trying to be selfless and giving. She was trying to be like Beth. And then he *really* got it.

It was the differences that made him love Fran exactly the way she was. It was her unique spirit that made her so special and dear. Did she love him, too?

Was that why she'd looked so devastated when he'd said he'd never asked her to change? Because she'd wanted to hear that she was already okay?

''You're right, Ma. I am a blockhead. I just hope it's not too late to fix it.''

* * *

With a breaking heart, Fran walked down the corridor to her apartment after a long day of not seeing Alex at work. In one hand, she clutched the long loaf of French bread she had bought at the market. She wasn't sure what she'd fix for dinner to go along with it. Maybe nothing. Carbs were the feel-good food.

And she desperately wanted to feel good, or at least better. Because in her other hand she held the letter of recommendation Alex's secretary had given her. Fran had realized in that moment how much she'd hoped that Alex would tell her he loved her and that he couldn't let her go.

"You're the world's biggest fool, Frannie Carlino," she said to herself.

She stopped in front of her apartment and juggled to free a hand so that she could get her keys out and unlock her door. When she went to insert it, the door inched open. Fear knotted her stomach. Was someone in there?

She jammed her letter in her purse and slung it over her shoulder, then wielded the loaf of crusty bread like a baseball bat as she slowly and quietly stepped inside. Listening intently, she heard what sounded like a muffled curse coming from her kitchen. A male voice. And she sniffed when a delicious smell drifted to her.

After peeking around the corner, she moved forward cautiously. When she made it to the doorway between the two rooms, she instantly recognized the man standing there.

"Alex!"

He turned around and a grin tugged at the corners of his mouth. He put his hands up. "You should put that down before someone gets hurt."

She wanted to brain him with the bread. He'd hurt her with something far more deadly than that. Words—or lack of them. Almost in a daze, she lowered her arm. "What are you doing here?"

"I need—"

"How did you get in?"

"The building manager—"

"What have you done to my kitchen?"

She looked at the mess he'd made. Several empty pasta boxes sat on top of the overflowing trash container, along with cellophane bags and plastic cartons. If she wasn't mistaken, the discards had held the ingredients of her original recipe. And again if she wasn't mistaken, he'd made it more than once.

"You've got some explaining to do," she snapped.

"If you'll stop interrupting me, I'll answer all of your questions."

She set the French bread beside her purse on the counter. "Okay. First things first—what are you doing here?"

"I'm your boss. I came to make you an appreciation dinner."

The word *boss* punctured the bubble of hope that had inflated inside her. "Why?"

"By definition, a gesture of appreciation denotes respect and admiration. I respect and admire you."

"If you wanted me to leave before my contract with the company is up, all you had to do was ask. I got the letter of recommendation. That sent a message loud and clear."

"I dictated that yesterday, right after you asked for it. My secretary transcribed it this morning, before I had a chance to delete it." He put down the wooden spoon he'd been holding and walked the few steps over to her. "I don't want you to leave."

"How did you get into my apartment?" she asked. Hadn't he already said? She couldn't remember. She was losing her mind along with her heart, and desperately trying to prevent that tiny little bubble of hope from inflating again.

"I charmed your manager."

"I'm going to have to have a chat with Elena." If her building manager had been a guy, Alex wouldn't have gotten his big toe inside her place. And what was the other thing she'd asked? Oh, yes. "What have you done to my kitchen? It looks as if you've made the same dish twice." She looked closer at the trash. "Nope. Three times. What gives?"

"It has to be perfect. For you."

Why? she wanted to shout. She wasn't perfect. She would never be like the woman he'd loved and lost. Why did he have to rub her nose in it?

She was so confused. "Is this about talking me into staying with the company? Or—"

"Both," he answered, a look in his eyes that turned her insides the same consistency as the angel hair pasta he'd overcooked in her six quart Dutch oven.

She didn't want to discuss the "or." That would hurt too much. So she went straight to business. "I can't stay with the company."

"Why not?"

Because it would break my heart to see you every day, to be *this* in love with you for the rest of my life, and know that you'll never be able to love me back.

"I just can't," she answered helplessly.

He walked over to her purse and grabbed the letter that was sticking out. "Marchetti's letterhead," he said, glancing at it. Then he met her gaze with an intensity that took her breath away. "To whom it may concern, Miss Francesca Carlino is the most gifted chef I've ever worked with. She is beautiful—"

"That's not in the letter," she protested breathlessly.

"—spirited, maddening, loving, and I would appreciate it if you didn't hire her so she would continue to work for me."

"Alex, I can't—"

He ripped the letter in half, then in half again.

"Why did you do that?" she asked, astonished.

"Because I won't let you go."

"I'm the wrong woman. No matter how hard I try, I will never be the right one. You said so yourself. You didn't ask me to change."

"Why would I do that when you're already the perfect woman? 'Don't change a hair for me, not if you care for me.'" He took her face in his hands and whispered, "'My funny valentine.'"

Then he lowered his mouth to hers. She rested her palms on his chest and gave herself up to the magic of his kiss. In spite of her self-warnings, hope blossomed inside her. He nibbled at her lips, softly, sweetly, until she grew hot all over.

She pulled back, and said breathlessly, "I care for you. But I couldn't change even if I wanted to. My mother made me see that. And also that doing for the ones we love is a privilege, not a punishment." She met his gaze. "I had a talk with my folks. Daddy says it's a guy thing. He wants me settled—to a man who will love me like he does my mother. And someone I love like she does him," she added.

"Do you love me?" Alex asked.

She saw anticipation in his eyes, the hope that she

would say yes. Whether or not he returned her feelings, she had to be honest with him.

"Yes," she answered simply.

He closed his eyes for a moment and nodded slightly as he breathed a sigh of relief. "Your fetching and carrying act showed me something, too."

"What?"

"It's about Beth," he stated. "I loved her and it hurt a lot when I lost her." He ran a hand through his hair. "But she wasn't the right woman to make me happy," he explained. "She was too perfect. At first I was in awe of that and flattered. I tried to meet her halfway. But with her there *was* no halfway. When someone gives everything and then some, it's overwhelming. And..."

"There's more?" Fran asked.

He nodded. "I realized that I didn't put off the wedding because of my career. I did it because I had serious doubts. Maybe subconsciously, but they were there, preventing me from taking the next step. If she hadn't died, we would have played our relationship out. I would have realized it was wrong."

"And saved so much guilt and pain," Fran murmured, her heart breaking for him.

He shook his head. "It's over now. Thanks to you."

"I don't understand what that has to do with me. You said from the beginning that Marchettis only get one chance at love."

"*True* love. That wasn't what Beth and I had. The moment I saw you, you brought light back into my life as no other woman could have. Your spirit breathed energy and sustenance into my withered soul. It scared me. I didn't want to care because it hurts too much when it's taken away. But being around you, it's impossible not to get caught up in your zest for living.''

"Really?"

"I love it when you fish for compliments." He grinned, then his expression turned serious. "Like limbs with restricted circulation coming back to life, my growing feelings for you were like pins and needles to the heart. It's normal to resist something that hurts. So I pushed you away."

"What are you trying to tell me?" She held her breath.

"I love you, Frannie Carlino. I don't care if you hate the nickname. It's cute, just like you. You're funny and wonderful."

"So are you, as much as I'd prepared myself that you wouldn't be." She curled her fingers into his shirt, holding on for all she was worth. "I was hiding, too, from the humiliation and hurt of being used. But I don't need your glasses to see that you're not like that. You're what I've always wanted and was so afraid I'd never find that I wouldn't even look."

He put his hands over hers. "Well, you've got me. I want you to marry me. Please say you will. Be my valentine forever and a day." He pulled her into his arms and held her so tightly it hurt. But it was discomfort she reveled in. "I promise that if you'll become a Marchetti, our marriage will be a fifty-fifty partnership."

How could she say no? Her mother was right. Fran could have it all. And the best part was that he was the man of her dreams.

"I would love to marry you, Alex. With everything I've got I love you and want to make you happy. Be your valentine forever and a day," she said.

"Thank God," he breathed against her hair.

His words put a glow in her heart that would last the rest of her life. Her spirit was restored, along with her pesky inclination to tease him.

"So, you want to make me a member of the family? And it has nothing to do with putting the Marchetti name on my original recipe?" she asked, pulling away just far enough to see his expression.

He grinned. "Maybe. Because I have very fond memories of that particular dish. Your very unique and special brand of dishing out kisses to negotiate is what made me fall in love with you. And so I have very selfish reasons for wanting to keep it—but mostly *you*—in the family."

He kissed her again, and she felt that she was the luckiest woman in the world. She had Alex. Together they had found that love was the secret ingredient in their own recipe for happy ever after.

* * * * *

#1 *New York Times* **bestselling author**

NORA ROBERTS

brings you more of the loyal and loving,
tempestuous and tantalizing Stanislaski family.

Coming in February 2001

The Stanislaski Sisters

Natasha and Rachel

Though raised in the Old World traditions of their
family, fiery Natasha Stanislaski and cool, classy
Rachel Stanislaski are ready for a *new* world of love....

And also available in February 2001 from
Silhouette Special Edition, the newest book in the
heartwarming Stanislaski saga

CONSIDERING KATE

Natasha and Spencer Kimball's daughter Kate turns her
back on old dreams and returns to her hometown, where
she finds the *man* of her dreams.

Available at your favorite retail outlet.

Silhouette®
Where love comes alive™

Silhouette —

where love comes alive—online...

your romantic escapes

Indulgences

♥ Monthly guides to indulging yourself, such as:

★ Tub Time: A guide for bathing beauties
★ Magic Massages: A treat for tired feet

Horoscopes

♥ Find your daily Passionscope, weekly Lovescopes and Erotiscopes

♥ Try our compatibility game

Reel Love

♥ Read all the latest romantic movie reviews

Royal Romance

♥ Get the latest scoop on your favorite royal romances

Romantic Travel

♥ For the most romantic destinations, hotels and travel activities

SINTE1

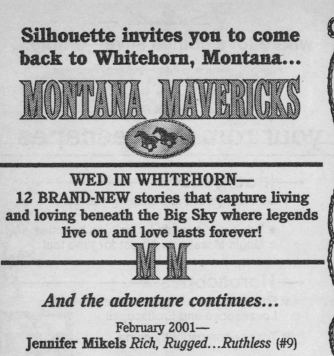

Coming in January 2001 from Silhouette Books...

ChildFinders, Inc.:
AN UNCOMMON HERO

by

MARIE FERRARELLA

the latest installment of
this bestselling author's popular miniseries.

The assignment seemed straightforward: track down the woman who
had stolen a boy and return him to his father. But ChildFinders, Inc.
had been duped, and Ben Underwood soon discovered that nothing
about the case was as it seemed. Gina Wassel, the supposed kidnapper,
was everything Ben had dreamed of in a woman, and suddenly he had
to untangle the truth from the lies—before it was too late.

Available at your favorite retail outlet.

Silhouette®
Where love comes alive™